"Do you believe this sky?" Nadine pointed at the stars above her and Lamont.

"I hope it's this clear tomorrow tonight," he said.

She looked at him, and sent his heart into overdrive. "Why?"

"Might be inclined to throw a couple of steaks on the grill…if you'll share 'em with me."

Nadine turned to face him. "Lamont London," she said, her blue eyes boring into his, "are you asking me out on a date?"

Suddenly, Lamont stared at the floorboards beneath his boots, trying to make sense of everything that was going on in his head and his heart.

"I like you, Nadine."

She reached over and gently squeezed his forearm. "And I like you, too. You've always been a good neighbor, and I count myself lucky to call you 'friend,' too."

Friend? The term made him feel like a schoolboy, because he wanted this to be so much more. He'd broken bones and tamed wild stallions. But something told him trying to woo Nadine might be his greatest challenge yet.…

Books by Loree Lough

Love Inspired

*Suddenly Daddy
*Suddenly Mommy
*Suddenly Married
*Suddenly Reunited
*Suddenly Home
His Healing Touch
Out of the Shadows
†An Accidental Hero
†An Accidental Mom
†An Accidental Family

*Suddenly!
†Accidental Blessings

LOREE LOUGH

A full-time writer for many years, Loree Lough has produced more than two thousand articles, dozens of short stories and novels for the young (and young at heart), and all have been published here and abroad. She is also an award-winning author of more than thirty-five romances.

A comedic teacher and conference speaker, Loree loves sharing in classroom settings what she's learned the hard way. The mother of two grown daughters, she lives in Maryland with her husband.

An Accidental Family

Loree Lough

Love Inspired

Recycling programs
for this product may
not exist in your area.

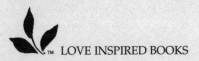

LOVE INSPIRED BOOKS

ISBN-13: 978-0-373-81553-1

AN ACCIDENTAL FAMILY

Copyright © 2011 by Loree Lough

www.LoveInspiredBooks.com

Printed in U.S.A.

And then I will welcome you, and I will be a father to you, and you will be My sons and daughters, says the Lord Almighty.
—*2 Corinthians* 6:18

Every time I watch the Oscars,
I empathize with the actors who try—
in a very short time span—to thank everyone
who made their careers and awards possible…
without leaving anyone out! I pray you'll
bear with me as I make the same attempt to
show my gratitude for the individuals
who helped *Accidental Family* come to pass:

My faithful readers (many of whom became
cherished friends over the years), my amazing
editor, Melissa (who knows a good story when
she reads one), the creative guys and gals at
Love Inspired (whose talents made this beautiful
cover possible), my real-life hero-husband
(whose support grows stronger and steadier
by the year), my loving daughters (for believing
in me even when I didn't), and their kids
(who provide thousands of "braggy grandmom"
moments), and Katharine Grubb
("The 10-Minute Writer," who shared a few words
that sparked an idea and solved a problem for
the heroine). Last, but certainly not least, to our
heavenly Father, who blessed me with a career
that allows me to enjoy every working moment
and allows me to share His word!

Chapter One

Lamont had never felt more alone in his life.

Strange, since the church bulged with longtime friends, family and neighbors, here by invitation to witness his youngest daughter's wedding.

They stood at the back of the church, just the two of them, waiting arm in arm for their cue to march toward the altar. Lily smiled up at him through the gauzy mist of her veil. "I love Max like crazy, Daddy," she said, tears shimmering in her big green eyes, "but *you'll* always be my best guy."

He wanted to tell her how beautiful she looked, that he was proud of the woman she'd become, that her mama would have been proud of her, too, but a sob caught in his throat. He patted her tiny, white-gloved hand and ground his molars together as those first strains of "The Wedding March" came through the closed chapel doors.

The roses and lilies of the valley in her bouquet began to quake, and he tried again to come up with something, *anything* that might calm and comfort her. But now the choking sob had made its way to his brain, making him feel just plain stupid as he continued patting her hand.

Then the doors opened, and a couple hundred parishioners turned simultaneously in their pews, smiling and craning their necks to get that first glimpse of the bride and her dad. Evidently, his hearing was pretty good for a guy in his fifties, because despite the window-rattling crescendo of the music, he could make out "Isn't she pretty?" and "He's so handsome in a tux," rushing down the aisle like an ocean wave.

Next thing he knew, Lamont found himself at the altar, lifting her veil, kissing her forehead… and handing her over to the young man who'd take care of his Lily from this day forth.

"Who gives this woman?" the preacher asked.

They'd practiced this, just last night, but Lamont didn't want to spout the two simple, one-syllable words they had assigned him. "She's *not* a woman," he wanted to shout instead, "She's my baby girl!"

But after his mechanical "I do," he walked woodenly to his seat, and sat tugging at the stiff collar of the tuxedo's white shirt, trying to pay attention as Lily recited her vows and exchanged rings with Max, trying not to blubber like a toddler when the bride and groom shared their first kiss as man and wife.

When they faced the congregation, Lily looked at him and sent a silent reminder: "*You'll* always be my best guy, Daddy…"

It put a lump in his throat and tears in his eyes, and Lamont tried to hide it by lifting his chin. But Lily saw and knowing what it meant, blew him a little kiss, the way she had since she was a toddler. And, as always, he pretended to catch it and tuck it into his pocket.

"Ladies and gentlemen," the pastor droned, "I give you Mr. and Mrs. Maxwell Sheridan."

All in attendance stood and applauded, including Lamont—though his heart wasn't in it. Because this was it. The end. Tonight, he'd go home to that big house, empty save the constant companionship of his ever-faithful mutt, Obnoxious.

An usher led Lily's mother-in-law to the back of the church. Georgia looked gorgeous, more content than he'd ever seen her. And why wouldn't she be, when Max had come home to Amarillo—this time to stay—and brought with him his formerly motherless little boy, Nate, and given her a daughter named Lily to love. Lamont supposed Georgia's new husband deserved some of the credit, and it made him wonder—if his new son-in-law's rough-around-the-edges mom could find a second chance at love, was there hope for him, too?

He took his place in the receiving line as the pastor's wife locked him in a grandmotherly hug. "Beautiful ceremony."

Behind her, his housekeeper, Peggy, said, "Beautiful *bride!*"

"Thanks," he told them. "Good to see you."

But not nearly as good as it was to see the pretty widow who owned the ranch next to his.

"Hey, good-lookin'," Nadine said. "I declare, you're more gorgeous than the groom." She looked down the receiving line where Max stood smiling at Lily. "And that's saying something!"

"You clean up pretty good, yourself." An understatement, he thought, admiring the knee-length azure sheath that accented her womanly curves and brought out the pale, glittering blue of her long-lashed eyes.

"This old thing?" Clucking her tongue, she fluffed the ends of her shoulder-length blond hair. "Why, I've had it for—" laughing, she stood on tiptoe to adjust the knot of his bow tie "—for exactly one day. Big sale down at Gizmo's," she added conspiratorially.

Nadine was nothing if not honest. Just one more reason to like her. Plus, she was one of the few people in his life who, by her very presence, could lift his spirits.

When she finished with the tie, she straightened the shiny black button-toppers that had come with his tuxedo, then tidied the pocket square in his breast pocket. It made him feel cared for and pampered, the way he had when Rose was still—

"See you at the reception hall," Nadine said. "Save a square dance for me, y'hear?" And with a flirty little wave, she disappeared into the crowd to wait her turn, blowing bubbles at the departing bride and groom.

His arms felt empty when she stepped away. Empty, and despite the dry Texas heat, a little bit cold.

Lily and Max, still in full wedding garb, joined the line of celebrants who made wings of their arms and beaks of their hands as the band played "The Chicken Polka."

"I need a break," Nadine said, plopping onto the chair beside Lamont. And waving a dinner napkin near her face, she laughed. "I'm so hungry I could eat a horse and I'm sweating like a pig." She stopped waving to add, "And don't *you* look like the cat that swallowed the canary. What's up your sleeve?"

"Not much, O Mistress of Clichés," he teased.

She gazed toward the dance floor. "They make a good-looking couple."

Lamont shrugged. "They'd look a whole better if they were somebody else's kids, two-stepping at somebody else's wedding."

She responded with a playful shove to his shoulder. "Take heart, *Dad*. I know what you're going through, 'cause I've been there, too. 'No one is good enough for *my* kid,'" she said, drawing quotation marks in the air.

She had it all wrong. Lamont liked his newest son-in-law just as much as he liked Reid, his oldest daughter's husband. "He's okay. I guess." His twins, Ivy and Violet, were living on their own, but Lamont felt fairly certain that when they chose life mates, he'd feel the same way about those young men, too.

"Yeah, 'okay,' but still not quite who you'd have chosen for her, right?"

She'd cocked her head to say it, and looked at him from the corner of her eye. He hadn't slept much last night, or the night before, for that matter. Maybe exhaustion explained why it seemed that Nadine was flirting with him.

The dance floor emptied as laughing, red-faced dancers returned to their seats. As the band eased into a waltz, Lamont frowned. He'd never much cottoned to ballads, especially if the lyrics spoke of lonely, broken hearts. Then Nadine started singing, and suddenly, he didn't mind as much. She had a soft, sultry voice that simultaneously soothed him and quickened his heartbeat. He wanted to hear more, up close and personal. So he bowed slightly and held out one hand. "May I have this dance?"

She followed his every step as though they'd been dancing together for years, when, in truth, he didn't think they'd shaken hands or shared a hello hug, let alone—

"Do you realize this is a first?"

He grinned. "Great minds think alike?"

"Beats the alternative…"

"Which is?"

"To quote my grandpa, 'Fools seldom differ.'"

And when she laughed, the invigorating sound showered over him like warm spring rain.

"So how's it feel…?"

He almost admitted that holding her this close felt so good that he wanted to kick himself for not asking her to dance before. Thankfully, he didn't get the chance, because she said, "…knowing you're finally on your own."

Lamont harrumphed. He'd just as soon forget that he'd gone a little nutty after Rose's death, escorting pretty young things around town two or three nights a week. A few years of that wore his patience thin, and since not a one of them came close to filling Rose's shoes, anyway, he hung up his eligible bachelor hat for good. "Please. Don't remind me."

Nadine patted his shoulder. "Now, now. Look on the bright side."

What bright side? He'd didn't like the dating scene and he didn't like the prospect of living alone. Especially not if it meant rattling around that big house, all—

"Think about it…total control of the TV remote, football 24/7, network news during supper…" She laughed again. "You'll probably turn into a couch potato or a hermit or something, and we'll probably never see you again!"

Oh, you'll see me, he thought. *You can count on it.*
Resting her head on his shoulder, Nadine sighed. "I'm only teasing. I remember how absolutely awful it was, going home alone that night when Adam married Julie. It took me weeks and weeks to get used to how quiet and empty the house felt."

"Hey, now *there's* a way to lift a guy's spirits," he said, chuckling.

One hand over her mouth, she cringed. "Oh, wow. Sorry. Guess I got my empathy and sympathy pills mixed up this morning."

The song ended and, for the second time that

day, he regretted having to let her go. His gaze followed her to the table where her son, granddaughter and daughter-in-law sat, and tried to figure out what to make of the feelings she'd stirred inside him.

Fingers, snapping near his ear, brought him back to attention.

"Earth to Dad, Earth to Dad…"

"Hey, Reid."

"Man," his eldest son-in-law said, "were you off in Never-Neverland!" He grinned. "Or should I say 'Nadine-Nadineland?'"

Lamont laughed good-naturedly. "Is it my fault if I have a good eye?"

"You can fool some of the people some of the time, but I'm not fallin' for that line of malarkey." Reid leaned closer. "Don't worry—your secret's safe with me."

Frowning, Lamont stiffened and glanced at the gaudy gold clock above the door. Two hours before the reception ended. Officially. Then there'd be gifts to pack into the car, and bills of lading to sign, checks to write and—

"Lily looks great today."

Reid was right about that. "I hate to sound like a braggart, but all four of my girls are knockouts." He found each one in the crowd. "Their mama would've been proud."

"Rose would have every right to be proud. Of them, and of you, too, because you did a bang-up job, raising them all by yourself." He shook his head. "Don't think I could've handled it."

Lamont met his eyes. "Sure you would have. What choice would you have?"

Cammi walked up to them, linked arms with both men. "So, what are my two best guys gossiping about?"

"I was just telling your dad what a great job he did, bringing up you girls."

She stood on tiptoe to kiss Lamont's cheek. "He's the best dad in Texas."

"In all of the Southwest," Ivy added.

"In the whole country!" Violet said.

"You're forgetting the universe," the bride put in.

"Knock it off," Lamont said, grinning. "You want somebody to snap a picture of me blushing like a schoolgirl?"

"Oh, I doubt anyone would confuse you with a schoolgirl."

Weird, Lamont thought as Nadine stepped up beside him, how natural and normal it felt, sharing this warm family moment with her.

When she smiled up at him, big eyes glittering like blue diamonds under the enormous crystal chandelier, Lamont had to control the urge to kiss her, right there in front of his girls. "So," he said to Lily, "what's next on the schedule? Cake cutting? Tossing of the bouquet?"

"Father-Daughter dance." Lily waved at the bandleader, who signaled the other musicians to end their song. The dance floor cleared, and in the ensuing hush, guests gathered at the edge of the parquet tiles. "Ladies and gentlemen," the emcee said into his microphone, "gather 'round as our host takes his best girl for a whirl around the floor."

Leave it to Lily to choose a song guaranteed to pluck his fatherly heartstrings. In the hope that banal conversation would distract him from the meaningful lyrics, Lamont told her again how pretty she looked. Talked about the wedding-perfect weather. Asked if she'd packed for the honeymoon, and if she'd remembered plenty of sunscreen and antiseasickness pills. "Careful not to stray too far from the beaten path," he warned, "because the news is full of stories about what happens when tourists end up on island backstreets." It seemed to be working, because he almost didn't see the huge circle of friends and relatives, standing all around the dance floor.

Almost…

As they two-stepped from one side of the room to the other, Lamont and Lily passed Nadine. Was he seeing things, or were those tears in her eyes? He would have turned to get a second look, if Lily hadn't chosen that moment to plant a loving kiss on his chin.

"Thanks, Daddy," she said, "for everything. You've made this the most special day of my life."

"Love you, Lilypad." The use of his pet name for her put a hitch in his voice, and he hoped she hadn't heard it.

"Love you, too."

The song ended, and the guests applauded, and his little girl ran off—to do whatever came next on her list of bridal obligations.

"Hey, sailor," Nadine said, taking his arm, "goin' my way?"

He shot her a grateful half grin and led her into the lobby. "Did I see you crying back there?" he asked when the doors closed behind them.

"Maybe," she said, blushing. "I guess. But only a little." And rolling her eyes, she playfully smacked his shoulder. "So what if I was?"

"Softie."

"Yeah, well, I saw a tear shining in *your* eye, too…"

"Yeah, well," he echoed, "I'm footin' the bill for this fancy shindig. I have every right to bawl like a baby!"

Had her laughter always been so melodious?

And why hadn't he noticed before that hearing it turned his ears hot and his palms damp?

She didn't look a day over thirty, though he knew for a fact that she'd turned fifty on her last birthday. *Hard to believe this woman's a grandma!* he thought, smirking.

"There you go again," she said, one well-arched brow high on her forehead, "looking like a cat with a mouthful of bird."

"A cat with a...a *what?*"

"Well, unless I wanted you to call me the Mistress of Clichés again, I figured I'd better come up with something original."

"Oh, trust me, you're original, all right."

Lashes fluttering, she blushed again. Yes, by golly, Nadine *was* flirting with him!

The banquet room doors opened a crack, and Cammi stuck her head out. "Dad, Lily is looking for you."

"Be right there." And once his eldest daughter was out of sight, he said from the corner of his mouth, "Guess it's time to write the check."

Nadine laughed again. "Nut," she said, kissing his right cheek.

He didn't remember much after that...

...except wishing she'd aimed a little *left*....

Nadine sat in the big wooden rocker, boot heels propped on the white picket rail surrounding the front porch. A little blustery to be outside so late on a February evening, but she didn't mind. She had fuzzy slippers, her favorite afghan and a cup of tea to keep her warm.

Behind her in the foyer, the dulcet tones of the grandfather clock sounded the ten o'clock hour. She ought to turn in, because tomorrow she was supposed to sing that new hymn she'd been practicing all week. But she wasn't the least bit sleepy.

Just five more minutes, she mused, closing her eyes to the starry, inky sky.

Smiling into the breeze, she admitted that this had been the best Valentine's Day in memory. Lily and Max made a lovely couple, their wedding one of the best she'd ever attended.

The startling jangle of the phone interrupted her peaceful reverie, making her slop tea over the mug's rim. "Rats!" she complained, standing. Well, at least it hadn't spilled onto her favorite blanket.

"Hey, Mom."

"Adam? Is everything all right with Julie and Amy?"

"We're all fine. Sorry to call so late, but I have a huge favor to ask you."

She slumped onto a counter stool and wrapped the telephone cord around her forefinger.

"For starters, I've been laid off. And thanks to Julie's math errors, our last eight rent checks have bounced."

Hopefully, he hadn't called to borrow money, because, much as she'd like to help them, Nadine barely had enough to meet her own bills this month.

"If I hadn't picked up when the landlord called tonight, I probably wouldn't have found out until I got home from work and saw all our stuff sitting at the curb. We're being evicted."

"Can't you can bargain with your landlord, explain things and promise to catch up a little extra with your rent every month?"

"That might have worked…*six months ago.*"

Julie had been hiding the bounced checks from him for that long? That didn't sound like the sweet girl his son had married. Nadine prayed she hadn't turned secretive because Adam had inherited his father's vicious temper, making her afraid to confess her mistakes. "Try not to be too hard on her, Adam. A thing like that…it could happen to anyone."

"Once or twice, maybe. But for almost a year?" He sighed into the phone. "Come on, Mom. Even you don't believe that."

No, she didn't. But her boy was already hurting enough. "So here's what we'll do," she said. "First thing in the morning, you kids will pack your car as full as you can, and once you get here, you can borrow my pickup for the rest. We'll store your furniture in the barn, and you know there's plenty of room for you here."

She could almost see him—one hand over the phone's mouthpiece as he relayed the information to his young wife. When Julie came on the line, her voice was thick with tears. "You're a lifesaver, Mom. A marriage saver, too. I—I don't know how we'll ever make it up to you."

Orphaned at eight, the poor girl had bounced from one foster home to another for years. It had taken a while to smooth the girl's rough edges, but in the five years the kids had been together, Nadine had come to love her like a daughter, and Julie's pain was almost as unbearable for her as Adam's. "You don't owe me a thing, honey. We're family, and this is what families do."

Her shaky sigh echoed through the phone line. "Still, I feel just awful that my stupidity put us all in this situation. Let me show my appreciation by doing the cooking and cleaning, and the laundry, too."

"Goodness, what makes you think you'll have the time and energy for all that after a full day at the dealership?"

A long pause, and then, "I—I lost my job."

Nadine didn't know what to say.

"The manager fired me, for an error…"

"An error that cost the company nearly $50,000!" Adam hollered from the background.

Nadine suppressed a gasp. Fifty thousand dollars! What in the world could be distracting Julie so badly! "Have you talked with the owner of the dealership? Maybe he'll overlook it, just this once?"

On the heels of a long, shuddering sigh, Julie said, "Wasn't my first mistake."

Nadine heard Adam, grumbling and growling in the background, and then Julie said, "Fine. Whatever. *You* talk to her, then, Mr. Know-it-all."

She'd worked hard to teach him to treat women with gentle respect, but Adam was, after all, his father's son, too. Maybe, their moving in would give her another chance to reinforce those lessons. But would the situation turn into the blessing in disguise people were forever talking about, or add fuel to the resentment already burning between them? Nadine had a feeling that, either way, she'd spend a lot of time on her knees in the weeks and months ahead.

Adam said, "She's got us in such muddle that we can't even afford to rent a truck, so thanks for the loan of yours. And for putting us up, too. I'll find a new job and get us out of your hair as fast as I can. Promise."

Had she ever heard him this angry? Nadine

didn't think so. But at least he had kept a lid on his temper. So far. *Lord,* she prayed, *help me say things that will defuse the situation.* "There's no hurry at all, son. I'm going to love having you home again!"

So, she thought after hanging up, these would be her last hours alone in the house. If these walls could talk, she thought, wandering the quiet rooms, what tales they would tell, about accusations and insults and violence.

Scowling, she shook off the ugly memories, focused instead on what needed to be done by morning. She'd give Adam and Julie the guest-room, and put Amy in her daddy's old room. And wouldn't the sewing room, with its nooks and crannies and sunny window seat make a wonderful playroom!

While dusting and vacuuming and putting clean sheets on the beds, Nadine had to remind herself that what the kids were going through was awful, and it couldn't have been easy, asking for her help. It would take some effort on all their parts to adjust to the situation, but by the grace of God, they'd manage. Soon, the kids would dig themselves out of their financial hole and find a new place to live.

"Just not *too* soon, Lord…"

Chapter Two

"Did you run over a nail or something?" Adam asked.

Squatting, Nadine inspected her right-front tire. "I suppose that's possible," she said, feeling for sharp objects. "But nothing seems to be sticking out."

As Lamont's pickup roared up the drive, she understood how those first residents of Texas must have felt when they heard the distant notes of the cavalry's bugle.

"G'morning," he said, climbing from the cab. His smile faded the moment he saw her flat tire. "What happened?"

"Everything was fine when I got home from grocery shopping last night," Nadine said, shrugging.

As Lamont stooped to get a closer look, Adam pointed at the gash in her right-front tire. "Found bootprints in Mom's rose garden, too, and they're way too big to be hers…"

"I probably ran over something inadvertently. As for those footprints, they're probably just Big Jim's," she said to Adam. "You know how much he likes flowers."

"I hate to say it, Mom, but you really oughta fire that guy."

"I know he seems a little…off, but Jim wouldn't hurt a fly." She laughed a little. "And I mean that quite literally. He's adopted several, you know."

Lamont and Adam exchanged an "Oh, brother" look.

"He's the hardest-working ranch hand I've ever had." She shrugged. "So he likes to keep bugs as pets and builds little cages for them. What's the harm in—"

"Mom," Adam interrupted, "no disrespect, but that's just plain weird."

"Adam's right, Nadine. That *is* weird."

Sighing, she looked at the cloudless blue sky. Could she make them understand? "Listen," she began again, "if he can be kind to a *bug* of all things, surely he wouldn't hurt me. Besides, he's worked here for years. Why would he start doing crazy things all of a sudden?"

"Would he even know if he hurt you?" Adam asked.

"Good question," Lamont added. "I mean, maybe he flattened the tire because he liked the hissing sound or something."

"Honestly, listen to yourselves!" Nadine scolded. "Jim's a little slow, but he isn't an idiot."

The men traded another "Uh-huh" look.

"And there isn't a mean bone in his body!" she added.

Lamont unpocketed his hands, pointed at the tire, then the flowerbed. "Now look, it's all well and good to believe in the innate decency of people, but you're carrying it to an extreme. Jim might be abnormal by some standards, but he's still a man. I've seen the way he looks at you."

"How…Jim?" The very idea inspired a nervous laugh. "Now that *is* crazy."

He looked to Adam for confirmation, and her son nodded in agreement. "If you insist on keeping him around, then you'd better keep an eye on him."

"A sharp eye," Lamont put in.

"Two against one ain't fair," she said. "I can take care of myself. It isn't as if I haven't had years of practice."

"Nobody who's known you longer than five minutes would disagree, but this is different."

"The boy's right," Lamont said, "on both counts."

Her two favorite men stood side by side. Why,

Adam had even adopted Lamont's stance, boots shoulder-width apart, arms crossed over his chest. She saw the resolute expressions on their faces. But they had nothing on her when it came to stubbornness. Or accurateness, either. Adam had only been home a few weeks. What did he know about Jim? And Lamont, well, he didn't know the man at all! Greeneland Ranch was hers and hers alone— land, stock and the mountain of unpaid bills— and she'd run it any way she saw fit, right down to whom she'd employ. "I won't fire him." Fists on her hips, she dared them to defy her.

"Oh, all right," Adam said, hands in the air. "I give up." He headed for the barn, saying over his shoulder as he went, "Good to see you again so soon, Mr. London."

"Same here, Adam."

"Speaking of seeing you," she said once her son was out of earshot, "what brings you to my place this early on a Sunday morning?" Hopefully, the subtle reference would remind him that this was her turf, and he wasn't in charge here.

"Just thought maybe you'd like a ride to church. Seems I recall something about your practicing for a solo before the services began."

Only Julie, Nadine's accompanist, knew about her rehearsal plans. "So my daughter-in-law is acting as my press agent now, is she?" Nadine grinned. "That girl might just turn out okay after all."

"After all?"

Julie was forgetful and clumsy, but she had a good heart, especially considering her troubled past. She waved his question away, unwilling to share that private bit of information, even with Lamont. "I'd love a ride into town," she said, "especially since I don't have a spare."

"I'll drive you to Lotsmart after church, and we can get one."

Between now and then, she'd have to come up with a legitimate excuse to avoid the side trip, because even at a discount store like Lotsmart, she couldn't afford a tire. "We have time for a cup of coffee, if you'd like."

"I'd like."

And maybe, between now and then, she'd figure out how to keep her heart from hammering every time he smiled at her, too.

Lily's Valentine's Day wedding seemed like only yesterday, but the wildflowers popping up everywhere—especially in Nadine's yard—proved otherwise.

Several times a week, Lamont had used one flimsy pretext after another to drive over there, telling himself that if she didn't intend to keep an eye on Jim, he would. Why, Lamont wondered, did Nadine's ranch hand occupy so many of his thoughts here at home, and rarely come to mind as he sipped coffee while her adorable granddaughter chased Julie's tabby cat around the kitchen?

Yesterday, he called to see if she wanted a ride to the church social. Normally, he didn't have time for such functions, but if it provided another bona fide reason to see her—and check on Jim—well, then, why not? She'd cited laundry on the clothes-lines and a sticky kitchen floor, critters that needed to be fed and weeds to pull in her flowerbed…and Lamont countered every excuse with one of his own. Thankfully, he wore her down.

He couldn't believe how fast the time passed as they stuffed themselves on baked ham and potato salad, talking with their fellow parishioners. Since Rose's death, his involvement at church had been limited to Sunday services, because everywhere he looked, his wife's contributions were constant re-minders of his widowhood. Oddly enough, despite all the hubbub, he'd had a right good time. The en-joyment continued as he drove her home, mostly because Nadine decided to rehash the squabble between Martha Turner and Barbara Gardner over whose vocal rendition of "The Old Rugged Cross" should be sung every Sunday. Dread and disappointment closed around him as his pickup ground its way up her gravel driveway. Had she invited him up to the house because she'd sensed it?

"It's such a pretty night," she said. "How about joining me for a cup of tea on the back porch?"

If she'd suggested guzzling it from a washtub on the roof, Lamont would have found a way to join her. Amazing, since the only time he'd allowed the stuff past his lips was the few occasions when he spiked a fever. Yet here he sat, toes tapping, fingertips drumming on the arms of his rocker as he waited for her to kick off her heels and brew the tea.

He looked around at her yard, colorful even in the semi-darkness. Bright spring blossoms shocked his senses. To him, planting involved seeds that became food for his livestock or turned out a couple of tomatoes and bell peppers for salad. Subconsciously, he compared it to his own lawn, devoid of blooms now that Lily was busy tending her own yard. Until now, he hadn't realized how much he missed the little things women did to turn a house into a home.

She handed him one of two steaming mugs. "You like yours black, right?"

"Smells like cinnamon," he said. How'd she know that, he wondered, when he couldn't for the life of him think of a time when they'd talked over herbal tea? Raising families and running ranches hadn't left much time for such niceties. Lately, though, he'd managed to make time for such niceties…lots of it. "I hope you don't mind my sudden intrusion into your life," he said as she settled into the other rocker. "You've made my adjustment to living alone a whole lot smoother."

"Oh, I'd hardly call you an intrusion."

He didn't know what to make of her slight hesitation. "What *would* you call me, then?"

Nadine leaned against the headrest of her chair, squinting as she considered her answer. His heart beat double time, waiting…

"I guess I'd have to say, you're a very pleasant diversion."

"From what?"

A strange expression—sadness? detachment?—flit across her features like a fast-moving shadow, and he wondered about that, too, as he waited yet again for a reply.

"Oh, just…everything."

She had a talent for turning two syllables into four, and three into six, just as Rose had. Lamont waited for the usual twinge of grief that followed a memory of his late wife, and when it didn't come, he chalked it up to Nadine's gift for making folks feel at ease.

"Do you believe this sky?" She pointed at the stars, winking on their bed of black velvet, then clucked her tongue. "And the so-called experts were calling for thunderstorms..."

"I hope it's this clear tomorrow night."

She looked at him over the rim of her mug, and sent his heart into overdrive. "Why?"

He shrugged. "Might be inclined to throw a couple steaks on the grill, if you'll share 'em with me, that is."

She put her cup down and turned to face him. "Lamont London," she said, her blue eyes boring into his, "are you asking me out on a date?"

He'd gone down the "dating road" more times than he cared to remember, with disastrous consequences. Granted, he was mostly to blame, comparing every woman to his wife a couple hundred times between the pickup and the dropoff. He'd made a promise to Rose after that last calamity: Since no woman could hold a candle to her anyway, why torture them and himself? "Can't a fella be neighborly without people jumping to conclusions?"

It was a moment before she answered, "Sure. I guess so."

"Sure," a fellow could be neighborly, or "sure," she'd share the steaks with him? "Can I take that as a 'yes'?"

She gave a one-shouldered shrug. "Why not?"

Chuckling, he said, "Try to curb your enthusiasm."

"Can't a gal be blunt without people getting overly sensitive?"

My, but he liked the sound of her laughter! But why stop there? He liked everything about Nadine, from her sunny blond hair right to the cherry-red toenails poking out from her terrycloth slippers.

Lamont stared at the floorboards beneath his boots, trying to make sense of everything that was going on in his head and his heart. He'd escorted a couple dozen good-looking women to the movies, dinner and concerts, and never once felt the way he did drinking tea with Nadine.

"I'm probably wasting my breath," he said, "pointing out that I'm not one to mince words."

"I've been in the crowd at enough cattle auctions to know *that's* the truth!" she said, grinning.

Lamont didn't have a clue what she meant. But that was no surprise, because what he knew about women, he could put in one eye.

She reached over the table between them and gently squeezed his forearm. "And I like you, too. You've always been a good neighbor, and I count myself lucky to call you a 'friend,' too."

"I like you, Nadine."

Friend? The term made him sound like a wet-behind-the-ears schoolboy, because he wanted this—whatever this was between them—to be so much more. And doggone it, he didn't cotton to feeling this way, not one little bit! He'd sustained broken bones taming wild stallions, and the ice-white scars on his forearms were reminders of his run-ins with barbed wire. The whole idea behind dating vain, empty-headed beauties was to ensure he'd never be tempted to marry one of them. But this thing with Nadine?

Show me a sign, Lord. Show me a sign!

The wind kicked up, thunder echoed in the distance and a bolt of lightning sliced the black sky. Coincidence? Or had God decided that it took the power of nature to get the message through his thick skull?

He didn't have time to come up with an answer because, quick as the blink of an eye, the skies opened up. Lamont could barely see his truck through the teeming rain.

"Oh, my," she said, standing to gather their cups, "you'd better make tracks, cowboy. You know what that road is like in a storm…"

Yeah, he knew. The hard-packed runoff would turn the blacktop into a swift-moving river of muddy water. But his place was just over the next rise. If he floored the pickup, he could make it home in ten minutes flat. Plenty of time to spend with Nadine—

Thunder boomed directly overhead and lightning exploded, brightening her yard.

Okay, Lord, I can take a hint...

"Guess I'd better make a run for it," he said, jamming the Stetson onto his head. "Thanks for the tea."

And as he hotfooted it toward his truck, he couldn't help but wonder if he was running from the storm flashing all around him...

...or the one roiling in his heart.

Chapter Three

Nadine tossed and turned for hours, alternately staring at the ceiling and punching her pillows. Flipping the covers aside, she stepped into her bedroom slippers and headed downstairs, belting a light terry robe on the way. No need for lights for, even in the dead of night she could navigate these rooms with her eyes closed. No surprise there, with all the practice she'd gotten while Ernest was alive. How many times, she wondered, filling the teapot with water, had she paced the floors, trembling with fear and rage and bitterness as she waited for the throbbing aches and pains of yet another beating to ease?

"Too many to count," she whispered, staring at the blue flame that she turned on under the kettle. She'd worked hard to keep the cuts and bruises camouflaged, a job made easier because Ernest had always been careful to leave evidence of his brutality in places that could be covered. If she didn't know better, she would have said he took those lessons from her own father.

When had the switch flipped, she wondered, turning Ernest from the loving young man who vowed to protect his sweetheart from her father's manhandling, to the mean-spirited husband who made her pa seem gentle as a kitten? A jagged scar on her forearm, the remnant of a long-ago beating, caught her eye. Instinct made her tug at the sleeve of her robe to hide it.

Old habits die hard, she glumly thought. If Nadine had a dollar for every time someone asked why she'd worn trousers and long-sleeved shirts in the dead of summer, maybe she could pay one of the steadily mounting bills that lay in a tidy stack on her desk.

These past three years had been tougher than any in memory. The run of bad fortune began when her stud bull broke free of his pen and wandered into the path of a speeding eighteen-wheeler. Two calves born that spring had been too weak to survive. The following fall, weevils had attacked her fields, destroying the harvest that would have fed the livestock. Then, three years of oppressive, unrelenting drought.

Somehow, Nadine managed to hang on through the first two years, even as other ranchers filed for bankruptcy. But this year? This year, her grip was slipping with each passing day.

She carried her tea outside and stood on the porch. The crisp scent of rain made her heart ache with dreary acceptance, because the steady downfall that now pounded the hard-packed earth had come weeks too late to save this year's crops.

Lamont's spread, by contrast, seemed untouched by nature's cruel hand. But then, he'd had the financial resources to dig deep wells that helped irrigate his fields. If one of his bulls died? Well, he had dozens of others grazing in white-fenced green pastures. Neighbors envied Lamont's knack for turning profits into wise investments. Some went as far as to ask his advice about where to put their money, when there was money left after filling their creditors' pockets. Nadine respected and admired Lamont's talents but, God help her, she envied them, too.

And envy was wrong. Spiteful and sinful. "A sound heart is the life of the flesh," she quoted Proverbs, "but envy the rottenness of the bones."

Shivering, she tilted her face toward the Heavens. "Lord, a little more backbone might be useful right about now."

Backbone. Lamont had it in abundance. Truth be told, it was his grit and his guts that she envied more than anything else.

Bowing her head, she hugged the thick ceramic mug to her chest. As the steaming brew warmed her face, she took a deep breath, pictured him sitting at her kitchen table, looking as though he belonged, stirring sugar into his cup with a spoon that, in his powerful, callused hand, looked like one from Amy's tea set.

Just thinking about him made her pulse race.

And she didn't welcome the reaction, either. Several times tonight, she would have sworn he aimed to kiss her, and the thought made her scramble for legitimate excuses to keep plenty of space between them, physically and emotionally.

She'd seen Lamont lose his temper—during cattle auctions, in the feed and grain, at the hardware store. Ernest personified the "street angel, house devil" rule; if Lamont behaved that way when people were around, how much more aggressive might he be one-on-one?

She couldn't afford to find out.

Nadine leaned against a porch support post as a mist of rain bounced up from the flagstone steps and onto her slippered feet. She barely felt it, though, as she thought of Rose. In all the years Nadine had known her, Lamont's wife hadn't given so much as a hint of being abused. But then, it wasn't likely Rose would have guessed what often went on inside Nadine's house, either.

Could she be wrong about Lamont? Did he fit the "His bark is worse than his bite" adage?

Not that it made a bit of difference. Nadine didn't trust herself to make smart decisions where men were concerned, so except for the few who worked for her at Greeneland Ranch, she'd avoided them altogether. And despite hard times, she'd held on as well as any male rancher she could name.

Shoulders sagging, she went back inside, bolted the door behind her and resigned herself to spending a few hours with the Good Book. God's word had helped her keep "white knight" dreams at bay in the past. By morning, any romantic notions about Lamont would be a distant memory, and she'd go back to accepting her lot in life.

But she didn't have to like it.

Bright and early the next morning, it was still raining when Adam padded into the kitchen, looking rumpled and frazzled as the weather outside. "Look at this mess," he said, stacking coloring books and construction paper on the table. He flopped onto a straight-backed chair as she closed her crossword puzzle book. "You can't even get a minute's peace and privacy since we invaded your house."

"You know I love having you…"

"It's only temporary," Adam said, "until Julie and I get this mess straightened out."

How many times had he said that since they'd moved in, weeks ago? *Lord,* she prayed, *help me find words to comfort him.* "I feel terrible admitting it," she said, sitting beside him. "But your cloud has been my silver lining. I haven't been this contented since before you and Julie got married and you left me all alone."

Adam chuckled at her deliberately exaggerated misery. "You're the best, Mom."

She'd been listening to her boy's laughter all his twenty-six years and knew when it was sincere and when it wasn't. Her heart ached for her only child. Maternal love hadn't protected him from measles or chicken pox; hadn't saved him from skinned knees, sprains and fractures; hadn't spared him the anguish of a breakup once he reached dating age. She couldn't protect him from this, either, but she aimed to try.

"Maybe while we're here," he said, "Julie will learn a thing or two from you about how to be a good wife and mother."

"Thank goodness I sent her to the cellar to sort laundry, because if she heard a thing like that, she'd be crushed. I'll admit she did some pretty ridiculous things, but you know in your heart she didn't do them on purpose. Why, the way that poor girl was raised, it's a wonder—"

"I'm tired of letting her off the hook because of her background."

She pressed a palm to each of his cheeks. "Julie is your wife, Adam, and the mother of your child. That money she lost is gone, but you can earn more. If you drive her away, well, you can't be sure you'll get *her* back. It's as plain as the nose on your face that she's trying. Give her credit for that, at least."

His expression reminded her of days long gone, when a shrug and a half smile were precursors to a bored "I guess you're right." This time, he got up and grabbed the lunch bucket he'd been carrying since he started that stock-boy job at Lotsmart.

He was halfway out the door when she said, "Will you do me a favor today?"

"Sure."

"Pray about what I said?"

"Guess it can't hurt," he said, his voice glum. "At least that won't cost me anything."

Every chance she got that day, she prayed, too. Nadine thanked God that neither the landlord nor the manager of the car dealership had decided to press charges against Julie, and for providing Adam with a job that helped put food on the table and keep the lights turned on. She asked Him to soften her son's heart toward his young, confused wife, and begged him to supply every dime required to keep the bank from foreclosing on her ranch. He'd seen her through bad times before, and He'd see her through this one, too. Nadine believed that. She *had* to believe it!

The jangling phone startled her, and she silenced it with a surly, "Hello…"

"Ah, a voice for sore ears…"

Was Lamont's voice really all it took to sweeten her sour mood?

"What time should I put the steaks on?"

Nadine had tossed and turned for hours, and by morning, convinced herself that she'd misread his signals. Why would a handsome, powerful widower be interested in a nearly broke grandmother whose kids had come home, adding to her wagonload of emotional and financial baggage? She came up with just one reason: He was the hero-to-the-rescue type and saw her as someone in need of rescuing. And when he tired of trying to fix what was wrong with her life, he'd move on to the next single gal waiting in the Available Bachelor line. By then, she'd be head over heels and it would hurt like crazy to send him packing. Far better to do it now, when all she felt for him was a tiny, schoolgirl crush. "How rude of me to wait until the last minute," Nadine began, "but—"

She heard his gruff sigh. "Don't tell me you're not coming to dinner…"

"Sorry, but I can't." Didn't dare was more like it, but she decided to keep that to herself.

The pause was so long and complete that, for a moment, she thought they'd been disconnected. Then Lamont said, "Is everything okay?"

Pursing her lips, she resisted the urge to say, "Jim hasn't killed any flies lately…that I know of." Stop being such a pessimist, she scolded herself. He's only asking out of friendly concern for you. "Yes, everything is fine."

"Guess you're just busy, eh, what with the kids home again and all. Well, here's an idea. How about if I bring the steaks over there? I have more than enough for—"

"No." If she sounded abrupt and cold to herself, how must she have sounded to Lamont? But it wasn't fair to punish him for the mess her life was in. Wasn't fair to assume that he was like Ernest, just because he'd shown signs of having a fierce temper. "It's just—I have a lot to do," she added, taking care to soften her tone. "Beds to make and—"

"No need to get all defensive with me, Nadine. I understand."

But his tone told her just the opposite.

"We'll do it another time," he added.

Was he waiting for her to agree, perhaps even suggest a day and time? Had she read him right, after all? The very thought filled her with fear and dread, because even if she hadn't made that ludicrous promise to herself, Ernest was the only man she'd ever dated. Besides, no way she could even begin to compete with the bevy of beauties who surrounded Lamont everywhere he went. "I—I'd better go," she said. "Julie volunteered to make supper, using an old recipe she found in one of my cookbooks. I promised to make her a list of the ingredients and—"

"Well," he interrupted, "better get a-move on, myself. But don't worry your pretty head about these thick juicy steaks going to waste. And don't give a thought to li'l ol' me, grilling and eating them all by my lonesome."

His good-natured teasing wafted into her ear, and she laughed softly. "When I say my devotions later, I'll be sure to thank God."

"For what?"

"For making you so big and strong and brave." Instantly, she regretted the coy comeback.

"Not so big and brave that I don't feel like a weak knobby-kneed young'un, missin' the daylights outta his best girl."

Nadine's heart ached. Because "what she wanted"

and "the right thing to do" were miles apart. "I'm sorry if you went to any trouble with—"

"Hey, you're no trouble, kiddo. No trouble at all." He paused. "But even if you were? Trust me, you'd be worth it."

Hang up, Nadine! Just hang up before you run over there and throw yourself into his arms! "Well," she muttered, "g'bye, then."

"See you soon, I hope," he said, and hung up.

And if Julie and Amy hadn't burst into the kitchen just then, she probably would have sat right down on the floor and cried like a brokenhearted little girl.

Because that's exactly how she felt.

Hours later, Lamont was still pacing his big country kitchen, head down and hands in his pockets.

Just last night, Nadine had seemed reasonably excited about his dinner invitation. What had changed between then and now? Had he violated some unwritten rule? Did she expect him to call sooner? More than once? "Women," he muttered, shaking his head. "The man who can figure 'em out will be a multitrillionaire for sure."

He grabbed a bottle of root beer from the fridge, pocketing the screw top as he strode into the family room. Settled in his recliner, Lamont picked up the remote and aimed it at the TV. The chair's well-worn brown leather squeaked in protest as he shifted his six-foot frame. Not even his favorite chair felt comfortable tonight.

Lamont pictured her as she'd looked last night, face aglow in the moonlight and blushing like a teenager as she reminded him that they both had to get up early.

"Doesn't take a brick to fall on my head," he'd joked. "I can take a hint."

"No," she'd said, giggling, "you can't. I've been dropping hints for the past hour!" Then, as if worried that she might have embarrassed him, Nadine said, "Drive safely. I'll see you tomorrow."

Well, it was tomorrow, and he didn't mind admitting to himself what a letdown it had been when she'd canceled on him.

Obnoxious padded into the room, rested his chin on Lamont's knees and whimpered. From the time he was a pup, the mutt had been attuned to his master's moods. "Don't worry, boy," Lamont said, ruffling his fur, "your old man is fine, just fine." He got to his feet. "How 'bout we fire up the grill? Who needs a woman around, changing her mind? Besides, we can't let perfectly good beef go to waste, can we?"

Obnoxious's ears perked up, and he answered with a breathy bark.

As Lamont flipped the steaks over the open fire, the dog sat watching, waiting patiently, grinning doggy-style. "Wonder if you'd be smilin' if you knew you were second choice as my dinner companion," Lamont said, cutting one steak into bite-sized cubes.

Obnoxious tilted his head, fuzzy brows rising as if he'd understood.

"Truth hurts, doesn't it, boy?"

The dog responded with a quiet yip.

Half an hour later, as Lamont scraped the bony leftovers of their meal into the trash can, he remembered the cool tone in Nadine's voice. Yeah, the truth hurt, all right, and hopefully, when he shaved in the morning, it wouldn't stare boldly back at him from the mirror.

The weeks dragged by slower than a donkey-pulled plow. Since Nadine had canceled "steak night," Lamont had been short-tempered with the ranch hands, and pretty much anyone else who crossed his path, too. His daughter, Lily, had a knack for teasing him out of a foul mood, but in good conscience he couldn't interrupt the new bride's zeal to get her house in order, especially not over something that was little more than a foolish infatuation.

Lamont gave some thought to changing Obnoxious's name to Oblivious, because if the mutt had noticed his master's beastly behavior, it sure didn't show. The dog ran circles around him now, leaping and yipping like a puppy as Lamont threw a blanket over the back of his favorite horse. "Long ride on a good horse will cure what ails a man," he said, cinching the saddle.

He'd barely slid his boot into Barney's stirrup when his cell phone rang. Lamont would've ignored it if it hadn't been Nadine's number on the caller ID. Instantly, his spirits lifted, as if a spring breeze had blown his foul mood deep into the dark and distant winter.

"Hey, there, pretty lady!"

A rascally chuckle crackled through the connection, telling Lamont what Adam needn't have said: "Sorry to disappoint you, Romeo."

He sounded so much like Ernest that Lamont instinctively shot back with a taunting remark, as he would've if Adam's father *had* made the comment: "If you've got nothing better to do than play with the telephone, c'mon over here. I'll be glad to—"

Laughing, Adam cut in. "Whoa, there. Easy, big fella."

Lamont could almost see him, grinning like a hyena, hands in the air as if he were the victim of a holdup.

"I'm just calling to see if you'll help us celebrate Mom's birthday tomorrow."

Birthday? But hadn't she just celebrated her birthday recently?

"Julie invited some of the folks from church, but mostly, it'll be neighbors. I've been scrimping and saving, but she's got some harebrained idea that this will show Mom how much we appreciate the way she let us move in here. And it just wouldn't be a party without Mom's best beau."

The term echoed in his head. He'd give just about anything if that were true, but Nadine's attitude when she canceled dinner echoed louder. Lamont took a deep breath, exhaled it slowly. "You're not too old to take over my knee, y'know." Just for good measure, he tacked on, "Whipper-snapper."

Adam snickered. "You've been saying that since I stood eye-to-eye with a rooster."

Lamont thanked God for old memories that, for the moment, anyway, blotted out Nadine's last phone call. The boy had seemed to prefer hanging around the ranch to staying home, and had enthusiastically performed mundane chores. The price to pay for Lamont came in the form of a few dollars—and pranks of every shape and variety. Adam had been about seven when he coated the door handle of Lamont's pickup with honey. The boy was eight or nine when he put salt in the sugar bowl. Once, he'd outfitted one of Lily's piglets in a doll's raincoat and hung a sign around its neck: "LONDON HOG." And after reading *Tom Sawyer* as a homework assignment, he tried to steal one of Cammi's fresh-baked cherry pies, cooling on the countertop. Startled when Lamont snuck up and seized his wrist, Adam's fingers pierced the crust. Instead of cringing or crying, the then-eleven-year-old grinned and shrugged. "Guess you caught me red-handed this time, Mr. London!"

If he'd had a son, Lamont would have wanted him to be just like Adam—bighearted and hardworking with a "Never say quit" spirit. "When's the party?"

"Tomorrow, Mom's house, three o'clock."

He'd earmarked tomorrow for mending fences and painting the front porch trim, but given a choice between chores and seeing Nadine?

"Be there with bells on."

"And carrying a bouquet of daisies?"

Daisies? As if he were *courting* her? "Adam, if I didn't know better, I'd think you were still a knock-kneed young'un instead of a grown man with a wife and daughter of his own."

He heard the grin in Adam's voice: "Remember what Mom says."

Lamont shook his head as Adam quoted her:

"God and nature have decreed that I must age, but I refuse to get old!"

He also remembered that, as a teenager, Adam had worked at the Flower Cart in town. "So," Lamont said, "if I wanted to bring roses, instead, what color should I buy?"

"Lemme see if I recall…" Adam cleared his throat. "White stands for purity, red means love, yellow is for friendship, pink is—"

He didn't hear anything after *love*. "Should I bring anything?" Lamont asked. "Beans? Ketchup?" He grinned. "Salt for the sugar bowl?"

"For an old guy, you have a pretty good memory." He quickly added, "Ladies Auxiliary is taking care of the food. Lily's making iced tea and lemonade, and Cammi's bringing the cake, so, thanks, but we're all set." Adam hesitated. "And just in case you run into her between now and tomorrow, Mom has no idea we're throwing this bash. I can hardly wait to see her face when everybody bellows, 'Happy Birthday'! She's liable to blow a gasket."

"Let's hope not. Remember what happened when my old tractor blew one."

The younger man chuckled. "Gave me nightmares for weeks. See you tomorrow," he said, hanging up.

"Well, Obnoxious," Lamont said, "looks like you 'n' me are goin' to a birthday party."

Sitting on his haunches, the dog cocked his head, as if to say *"I'm* invited?"

"Yeah, you can come," Lamont said, hoisting himself onto his horse Barney's back, "but only if you promise to coax Nadine into a corner so I can give her a birthday kiss."

Obnoxious stared for a moment, then woofed his consent and raced alongside the horse. Lamont led it in a gallop toward the back pastures. "You arrange that for me," he added, "and I'll grill up the thickest filet mignon in the freezer, just for you."

The dog stopped running so fast that dirt and grit spewed out behind him. Standing stock-still, he blinked up at Lamont, doggy grin as big as ever, then ran full speed toward the house.

Lamont leaned forward and patted the horse's mane. "Barney, m'boy, sometimes I think that mutt understands every word I'm saying."

By Lamont's count, there were at least sixty people in Nadine's backyard, mostly women, but none compared to the birthday girl. Not even his gorgeous daughters—and that was saying something.

He hadn't been able to take his eyes off her since she stepped off the back porch and slapped both dainty hands to her cheeks. "I can't believe it!" she chanted half a dozen times. "How'd you guys pull this off without me knowing about it?" The surprise turned her cheeks bright pink, making her look more like a college cheerleader than a grandmother.

She'd pulled her shoulder-length blond hair into a ponytail and secured it with a ribbon that matched the blue of her eyes. White sneakered feet seemed too tiny to hold a full-grown woman upright and, in his opinion, her jeans-clad legs were way too curvy to belong to *any* woman over twenty-one. Nadine topped off her outfit with a bright white T-shirt that said, "Beware: Picture-packin' Granny."

She was like a female Pied Piper, with no fewer than half a dozen tots hugging her knees, tugging at her pockets. As she balanced a chubby baby on one curvy hip, she held a toddler by the hand. Obnoxious pranced around, waiting for a pat on the head, and Julie's cat wove figure eights between Nadine's ankles. Yet amid all the squealing and giggling, barking and meowing, she smiled serenely, which only made her more beautiful to Lamont.

Woman like that should've had half a dozen kids, Lamont thought. Funny, but until that moment, he'd never wondered why she and Ernest quit after just one. Adam had been a handful, to be sure, but if Nadine could control this mob at the age of fifty-one, surely she could have handled two or three young'uns while she was in her twenties.

She looked up just then, and as their gazes locked, Nadine smiled and waved with the only appendage left: her pinky. Immediately, his heart started knocking against his ribs. What was it about her that could set his pulse to pounding and his palms to sweating? Not even his wife had been able to do that, and he'd loved Rose with all his heart.

Nadine's granddaughter darted up to Lamont and grabbed his hand. "Will you push me on the swing, Mr. London?" Without waiting for an answer, the four-year-old led him toward Nadine's wraparound back porch. "Grandmom's swing is too big. I can't get it going all by myself."

As if in a daze, Lamont followed the tiny blonde, then lifted her onto the wide, slatted seat.

"Do you like my new dress?" she asked, smoothing her frilly pink skirt.

"You're purty as a baby duck," he drawled, winking.

Amy gave him a sidelong glance. "Are baby ducks pretty?"

"*All* babies are beautiful."

As she considered his response, the breeze lifted blond bangs from her forehead, exposing a smattering of tiny freckles. Strange, but she looked more like Nadine than Adam or Julie.

"Do you think Grandmom is pretty?"

"Just between you and me," he said, looking to see if the coast was clear, "I think she's one of the most beautiful woman I've ever had the pleasure of laying eyes on."

"Flattery will get you anywhere."

He'd recognize that voice in a crowd at New York's Penn Station. Straightening, he turned, hoping she'd blame the heat in his cheeks on the warm afternoon sunshine. "Nadine, how long have you been standing there?"

Hooking thumbs into her belt loops, she bobbled her head. "Exactly long enough." Then, to Amy, "I'm gonna cut the cake soon, sweetie. Better wash your hands!"

In the blink of an eye, the child was halfway across the yard. "Don't worry, Grandmom," she hollered over her shoulder, "I won't slam the door on the way inside."

"Good girl!" Nadine called back. She cast a glance at Lamont. "She's a pistol, that granddaughter of mine."

"It's in the DNA, I reckon," he said, chuckling

as the back door banged shut. "Time to cut the cake, you say?"

Nodding, she began walking toward the paper-covered folding table that held an assortment of desserts. "How long did you know about this shindig?"

"Since yesterday afternoon, when Adam called to invite me."

"That's what everyone has been saying. He pulled this thing together awfully fast."

"I got the impression it was Julie who did most of the organizing. And it's high time you learned to let people do nice things for *you* once in a while."

He'd learned decades ago that Nadine didn't accept compliments well, that she preferred giving to taking.

"This is Adam's home. Julie and Amy's, too. I'm thrilled to have them here, even if it is only temporary."

"Is it?"

Her brow furrowed as she hung her head and sighed heavily. "I hope so. They have some serious money troubles, but…" She bit her lower lip. "Grace Mevers says I should open the presents, but I'd rather not."

Lamont chose not to press her for more details. Her kids' financial situation was none of his business, after all. "Because you want to open them after the cake and ice cream?"

"I don't want to open them *at all,* because what about those folks who couldn't afford to bring a gift? This was so last-minute. And everybody's lives are so busy. Surely some people didn't have time to bring a gift." She exhaled a sigh. "I'd hate for anyone to feel uncomfortable."

Lamont chuckled and, draping an arm over her shoulders, fell into step beside her. "Nadine Greene," he said, kissing her temple, "you know what your biggest problem is?"

"I don't like birthday parties?"

"Nope."

She looked up at him, a half grin on her face as one brow rose with teasing suspicion. "What?"

"Your heart is bigger than your head, that's what. And I love that about you."

He felt her stiffen against him when he said that, and for a reason he couldn't explain, it cut him to the quick. "Just so you'll know, I intend to be the last guest to leave."

"Oh?"

He loved the way she moved her delicate hands and batted those thick eyelashes. Fact was, he loved a lot of things about her—things he hadn't really noticed until lately. "Because," he said, "I have something for you. It's in the truck."

A little gasp passed her lips as her eyes widened. "Lamont, you didn't have to—"

"I know. I *wanted* to."

She glanced at her watch, and he could almost read her mind: In an hour, maybe two, the party would be over and she'd be faced with Lamont and his gift. Alone.

Would that really be so terrible?

Her friend, Grace, stood grinning alongside the rest of the partygoers, ready to strike a big kitchen match. "Don't light *all* those candles," Nadine warned. "They'll see the smoke all the way in town and send the fire department!"

Time dragged for the rest of the afternoon, and he wondered how she'd behave when her guests had all gone home. Would she treat him with welcoming warmth, as she had the night when they walked hand in hand around her yard, or with aloofness, as she had on the phone the night after?

Lamont shook his head and focused on the friends and neighbors who'd gathered around her. They pressed close, singing a loud, off-key rendition of the birthday song.

Everyone but Lamont.

There she stood, glowing brighter than the candles on her cake, blue eyes wide and smile sparkling, looking more gorgeous than any woman had a right to.

And here *he* stood, admitting, finally, that he wanted to be more than her friend and neighbor.

A whole lot more.

Chapter Four

With the sunset, the last of Nadine's guests crunched down her narrow gravel drive. As she'd thanked them for the birthday gifts and wished each one a safe trip home, Lamont sat in a rocker on her front porch, her sleeping granddaughter cuddled in his arms.

He couldn't say exactly when Amy had crawled into his lap, toting a shaggy purple teddy bear. Lamont glanced down at her rosy cheeks and grinned. Long enough for his arm to go numb, anyway. The dull ache seemed small by comparison to the warmth swirling in his heart. It had been a long time since he'd held his own girls this way, and much as he loved what wonderful women they had become, he missed moments like these.

Amy's steady, restful breaths soothed him. Heavy-lidded himself, Lamont leaned his head against the chair back and closed his eyes. When she sighed and snuggled closer, instinct made him press a soft kiss to her temple.

"If this isn't a Norman Rockwell moment, I don't know what is."

Without opening his eyes, he slurred drowsily, "I'd rather it was a Maxwell House moment."

"There's bound to be some left in the coffeepot. Want me to pour you a cup?"

Lamont peered at Nadine through a slit in one eye. She'd pulled out her ponytail, and her golden hair now swung freely around her slender shoulders. Silhouetted by the porch light, he could see every womanly curve. Man, but she was a good-looking gal, even after a long day entertaining guests, their kids *and* their pets. "What time is it?"

"Time to fix you a nice hot cup of coffee."

He wanted to tell her to sit with him, instead, but she'd already disappeared inside, like a wisp of smoke blown to the four corners by the spring breeze. Funny, he thought, how in the moment she'd stood there, close enough to touch, the very atmosphere had crackled with excitement. Odder still the knowledge that since she'd left, the air was quiet and still, reminding him of the hush following a thunderstorm. The comparison confused him, because he'd never felt anything but calm and comfortable in her presence. Lamont would have shrugged at the contrasts, if he wasn't afraid of waking Amy.

Nadine put two big earthenware mugs on the red gingham-covered table between the rockers. "You'd better hope this little nap doesn't keep her up all night, or you'll have Julie to answer to."

"If this li'l munchkin gives you any trouble, feel free to call," he said, winking. "As you can see, I'm great with kids."

Doing her best to hide a grin, Nadine crossed both arms over her chest. "You might be sorry you said that, at three o'clock in the morning."

"Hey, I put in my share of sleepless nights back in the day."

"I'm sure you did, what with four kids born one right after the other."

Her expression softened as she tilted her head, and Lamont would have given ten bucks to know what was going on in that head of hers. He didn't have time to figure it out, because Nadine moved closer and, bending at the waist, put her face mere inches from his.

Disappointment cloaked him like a cool fog when she gently lifted Amy from his arms.

"I'll just get her tucked in," Nadine whispered. "If you have to leave before I get back, I'll understand."

He hid his discouragement at her not-so-subtle

hint behind a slanting grin. "You can't get rid of me that easily. Your birthday present is still on the backseat of my pickup, and I'm not goin' anywhere 'til I see you open it."

"Well, you're more than welcome to wait inside." She glanced around the darkened yard, her gaze resting for an instant on paper cups and empty soda bottles. "It's getting kinda chilly out here."

When she stepped inside, Lamont grabbed the trash can she'd put on the porch earlier, and dragged it down the flagstone steps. If he knew Nadine, she'd be up there for half an hour or more, getting her sleepy-headed grandchild cleaned up and into pajamas, listening to her prayers, maybe telling her a bedtime story or two. More than enough time for him to get some of the party remnants cleaned up.

He tossed empty potato salad and cole slaw tins into the bag, then put what remained of the birthday cake on her kitchen counter. That done, he stacked her gifts on the living room sofa, placed her birthday cards on the coffee table and, with nothing left to do, headed back to the porch. When he hit the foyer, the distant strains of a familiar lullaby wafted down the stairs, stopping him dead in his tracks.

He followed it up the steps to Amy's room. Her voice was so lovely, soft and dulcet and the slightest bit husky. But then, he'd be hard-pressed to name something about her that *wasn't* lovely.

Was she sitting on the edge of Amy's mattress, he wondered, or in a stiff-backed chair next to the bed? When Lamont peered around the corner, it didn't surprise him to see Nadine stretched out on the mattress with Amy nestled happily in the crook of her grandmom's arm.

He smiled, then remembered the flat, rectangular package still sitting on his backseat. Tiptoeing down the steps, he headed for the driveway, hoping she'd like his gift. Something told him he'd never know for sure because, earlier, he'd watched her fawn over a gaudy clay refrigerator magnet the church organist had sculpted for her, seen her fuss over the sweater vest Marian the librarian had crocheted from pea green and purple angora.

Lamont sat in the rocker on her porch, the present in his lap. The coffee was cold now, but he sipped it anyway, enjoying every swallow because Nadine had made it for him. He felt at ease here, inhaling the aromas from her potted plants, looking out over the expanse of freshly mowed lawn, listening to crickets and night birds that filled the darkness with harmonious song. He could picture himself whiling away the evening hours with her, right here on this porch, chatting until it was time to turn in.

"I do believe this is the first time I've seen a tough cowboy with a pink bow on his belt."

He looked down. The way the gift rested in his lap, it did appear that he'd worn a fancy ribbon in place of a belt buckle. Laughing, he sat up straighter as she settled into the rocker beside him. "It isn't much," he said, handing her the little box.

"You shouldn't have, Lamont."

"Sure, I should. Gal doesn't turn thirty-five every day."

"Flatterer," she said, and carefully removed the ribbon. "Did you wrap this yourself?"

"Can't you tell by the wrinkles and the tape hiding the rips?"

"I really hadn't noticed," she said, lifting the box top.

Nadine parted the tissue paper and peered inside. "A gift certificate?" Turning it over in one hand, she read, "Dinner for Two at Cowboy Joe's, Best Steak House in Texas." She bit her lower lip before meeting his eyes. "Lamont, you shouldn't ha—"

"Sure, I should," he said again. Shrugging, he added, "I just thought, well, I kinda hoped you'd use it to treat me to a steak dinner." He grinned. "You know, to make up for canceling steak night."

Nadine tucked the card back into its tissue-paper

bed, replaced the lid, and sat the gift on the table beside Lamont's half-empty coffee mug. "Thank you."

Was she blushing? And why on earth was her lower lip trembling? And was that a tear glistening at the corner of her eye? Last thing he wanted to do was upset her. Presents were supposed to make people happy, not make them cry. "Nadine," he said, reaching across the space separating them, "it's your gift. I was only kidding. Take anyone you please to dinner at Joe's."

Nadine patted his hand. "It's a wonderful, thoughtful gift," she interrupted, "and I can't think of anyone I'd rather share it with than you."

Did she mean it? He stared deep into her big blue eyes. Well, it sure looked like she'd meant it. So then, why the waterworks? Sighing, Lamont prayed for a sliver of knowledge to help him understand this remarkable woman.

"And thanks for cleaning up the yard. You didn't have to do that, either."

He shrugged again. "No big deal. Saves you having to do it tomorrow."

She laughed. "Yeah, leaving me plenty of time to muck the stalls and shovel out the henhouse."

Lamont turned her hand palm up, traced his thumb over well-worn calluses, like connect-the-dots. If she were his woman, he'd see to it that she never had to work so hard. She deserved to be pampered and spoiled, to have her every wish fulfilled.

Instinct propelled him forward, where he knelt beside her chair. Automatically, his arms slid around her waist, and he drew her close. "Happy birthday, darlin'. I hope you have at least a hundred more, each one happier than the last."

Nadine bracketed his face with those hardworking little hands. "You're a smooth talker, Lamont London," she said, smiling softly, "but thanks for the well wishes, all the same."

"Ah, Nadine," he rasped, "you're wrong. That wasn't some practiced line. I meant every word."

She studied his face for what seemed like an eternity, analyzing his brow, his cheeks and chin, his mouth, as if trying to imprint it on her memory.

"You'd better cut that out," he warned, his voice foggy with emotion.

"Why?"

"You know why."

Her hands were still pressed to his cheeks, her eyes still boring deep into his when Julie called from the kitchen. "Mom, what do you want me to do with this leftover cake?"

"That girl has terrible timing," he groaned, sitting on his heels.

"Just leave it there for now," Nadine called out, as he returned to his rocker. "I'll take care of it later."

She got to her feet, held her hand out to him. When he gave his to her, Lamont looked at their entwined fingers, thinking how terrific it would be if their lives could overlap this way. Standing, he kissed her work-worn knuckles. Oh, how he cared for this woman, probably more than was good for either one of them right now. But too late for second guesses.

Not knowing what to say next, he let her lead him down the flagstone walk toward his pickup. She stepped back and waved as he slid behind the wheel and, as he drove off, he could see in the rearview mirror that she'd returned to the porch, where she stood on the top step, watching.

Lord, he prayed, *if she doesn't feel the same way, get me outta this before it's too late.*

The porch swing moved slowly, propelled by one well-worn boot heel. Lamont stared past the hip-high stone wall surrounding the terrace, beyond the row of long-spent daffodils and tulips that ringed the granite patio, hands wrapped around a cool brown bottle of root beer. A nippy late-spring wind rustled tree leaves and carried the scent of newly sprouting cow corn.

Lamont remembered how Rose had insisted that these maple trees would die, planted just beyond the porch. But knowing how much she loved reading in the shade, he'd mixed fertilizer and peat into the sandy Texas soil and made a point of getting up sooner than usual every day to water the spindly saplings, how he'd knocked off work a few minutes early to drench them again each evening. His efforts had paid off, because the trees had grown tall and sturdy, reminding him of how he'd often come in from the pastures and found her reclining in her favorite chaise, poring over a paperback novel or woolgathering about one thing or another.

Soon, her precious roses would bloom, as they had every spring since her death. He'd teased her dozens of times for doubting the maples could survive, because her prickly shrubs produced thousands of colorful blooms in the same hard-packed earth. "I didn't do it with smoke and mirrors," she'd say. "Hard work and sweat is the only way to earn blue ribbons!" Every spring, Lamont secretly hoped they hadn't survived the winter, because he sure as shootin' didn't need the constant reminder of her. But despite harsh weather and neglect, they came back, gorgeous and determined to stay alive.

Their natural stubbornness reminded him of

Nadine, who had outlasted life's hard knocks without looking any the worse for wear. Taking a deep breath, Lamont frowned and shook his head. He hadn't felt this rattlebrained since that day when he first saw Rose in Amarillo. He'd been a cocky young buck back then, so the notions whirling in his head and the feelings pounding in his veins hadn't surprised him. But now? At his age? What fifty-five-year-old man gets double-quick heartbeats looking at a grandmother?

"Sure doesn't look like any gran'ma I ever saw," he told Obnoxious. Sure, there were a few laugh lines on her pretty face, a hint of gray at her temples, but these things only made her more all the more beautiful, because they were confirmation of a life fully and well lived.

His gaze went beyond his fields, to her ranch. He leaned slightly to get a better view. Funny, but he'd never noticed before that the light from her house was visible all the way over here.

The thin-necked bottle slid from his hand and landed with a foaming, spattering *thud* between his boots as he leaped to his feet. The glow wasn't steady and calm, like the subtle halo of table lamps and porch lights. Rather, it ebbed and waned, brightened and dimmed.

Like fire?

Lamont didn't bother to lock the back door.

Didn't stop to wonder whether Obnoxious would follow. Grabbing his keys as he raced toward the pickup, he prayed that the golden ring of light was a brush fire. Because if the luster on the inky horizon was fire at her place, it had to be one hungry blaze to be visible from miles away.

Thankfully, he'd left his cell phone on the passenger seat. Grabbing it, he dialed 911. When the efficient, no-nonsense voice came on the line, Lamont barked out Nadine's name and address. "Better get a-move on," he growled. "Looks bad, real bad."

Lamont haphazardly tossed the phone aside and floored the gas pedal. If a Texas Ranger or a state trooper pulled him over, so much the better. The cop could provide a police escort, radio the fire department for more backup—

The breath caught in his throat as he finished the thought: and an ambulance.

Lamont tried to concentrate on the road, but the nearer he got, the more intensely the night sky above Nadine's house glowed. Her house was clearly on fire, as evidenced by the cherry-red and icy blue flames that licked the coal-black Heavens.

He found himself wishing, as he bulleted up her driveway, that it had been the barn ablaze— any outbuilding—instead of the house she'd spent decades turning into a home. A spray of gravel spewed out behind him as he stomped on the brake. He leaped from the cab without bothering to slam the door. "Nadine!" he yelled, tearing across the lawn. "Nadine!"

He bellowed Amy's name, and Adam and Julie's, too, but all he heard in response was the hissing and popping of the hungry fire as it gnawed at the clapboard siding.

If God heard his prayers, Lamont would find her out back, cussing and kicking dirt while aiming a garden hose at the fiery beast. His heart sank as he rounded the corner, for she was nowhere in sight. She'd parked her car in the usual place, he'd noticed earlier, beside Adam's seen-better-days pickup. The little truck was gone. Maybe no one had answered because they'd driven into town. Hadn't he heard Amy asking for a chocolate shake earlier? The thought gave him hope.

But it was nearly midnight. Even if the family had gone to Amarillo, wouldn't they be home by now? And then he remembered that Nadine had tucked Amy in, hours ago...

"Nadine!" he shouted, pounding on the door. "It's Lamont!"

But in place of her familiar voice, he heard only the crackling and sizzling of the fire, the frenzied howl of herd dogs, the neighing of alarmed horses and the bleating of Nadine's pygmy goats. Dread drummed inside him, because if she and her kids were in there…

The thought was too horrible to complete. He swallowed, hoped they'd gone to town. Anything—a flat, a stalled motor, a thrown rod—was better than the alternative.

Flames belched from the upstairs windows. Glass shattered and rained down on him like hail, each shard stinging his cheeks and forearms. The roar was deafening as fire gobbled at the shutters, folded over the eaves and climbed onto the roof.

Terror drove him, because if they were up there, they didn't stand a chance. He climbed the flagstone steps of her back porch and, leaning back, kicked the door for all he was worth.

Arm bent to protect his eyes from the blinding light and skin-crisping heat, Lamont spotted the cake plate he'd put on the table hours before. Shiny red ceramic splinters lay scattered across charred floorboards that once gleamed like spun honey.

Then he saw what looked like a pair of size five tennis shoes on the floor beside the pantry. *Nadine's* shoes.

And she was still in them.

Heart beating like a war drum, he plowed through the thick smoke, scooped her up and bolted toward the still-open door.

But the blast of air that followed him inside had built a hulking wall of scarlet flames between him and the exit, and raked the ceiling. To reach the safety of her yard, he'd have to break through it, carrying Nadine.

Soot ringed her nose and mouth. Was she breathing? He couldn't tell, and there was no time to check. If he didn't get her outside, pronto, only the Almighty knew what might happen.

Eyes squinted against the blinding brightness, he tucked her hands between his chest and hers, then pressed her face into the crook of his neck. Taking a deep breath, Lamont gave a mighty cry and surged ahead.

As he plunged through the fiery barricade, the thunder of the blaze melted into searing heat. He felt its fury, biting at his forearms and knuckles, his earlobes. The foul-smelling scent of burning hair assaulted his nostrils as he ran for his life and Nadine's. Legs churning, boots pounding—first over hardwood, then flagstone, and finally onto the welcoming softness of soft sod—he ran.

He'd gone halfway down her driveway before his legs gave out. Draping her across his lap, he gulped air and checked her pulse. Grateful tears brimmed in his eyes once he saw that she was breathing—raggedly, but breathing! "Hey," he whispered. Finger-combing burned bangs from her forehead, he cleared his throat, hoping she hadn't heard the hitch in his voice. Gently stroking her soot-streaked cheeks, he said again, "Hey, give me a sign you're okay, will ya?"

Long lashes fluttered, then her lids lifted, exposing blue eyes made violet in the fire's eerie orange light. "You kicked in my door," she croaked. "Bet ya busted the lock."

Blessed relief surged through him at the sound of her smoky voice. He hugged her tight. "Don't worry. I'll fix it." He heard her smack her lips, and wished he'd thought to grab the bottle of water standing in the cup holder of his truck. Then it struck him like a two-by-four to the head. "Where are Adam and Julie and Amy?"

"They…the kids took Amy…" She sputtered. "Drive-in movie," she said, "in…somewhere off Route 27, I think…"

"Thank God," he said, and as the welcome sound of sirens screamed closer, Nadine slid back into unconsciousness.

The ambulance was the last truck to screech to a halt. EMTs shoved him aside and lost no time hooking Nadine up to an IV, loading her onto a gurney and sliding her into the back of the vehicle. Lamont was telling a state trooper what little he knew about the situation when the rescue vehicle sped away, Nadine in tow.

Should he wait here for her kids or follow the ambulance?

A hand on his shoulder made him lurch.

"Sorry," a paramedic drawled, "didn't mean to startle you." Then, "Don't worry. I've seen smoke inhalation dozens of times and I know when it's bad. She'll pull through just fine. Besides," he added, chuckling, "that's no ordinary woman in the back of that truck. That's Nadine Greene. Me 'n' Nadine—we go way back." He took off his helmet and gave a slow nod. "Why, that li'l gal is stronger'n most men I know. The docs'll probably hafta tie her down, but mark my words, one night in the hospital, an' she'll be rarin' t'get out."

He'd meant to reassure, Lamont knew. And what he'd said was true—if anyone could rally from a thing like this fast, it was Nadine. But that thought was lost amid others: What kind of relationship did she have with this guy, and why hadn't she told Lamont about it?

He ran both hands through his hair as guilt churned in his gut. This was neither the time nor the place to be acting jealous that his steady girl might've flirted with the high school quarterback.

The firefighters all but had the blaze under

control. Water from their hoses spat and hissed as it pounded down on the smoldering remains of the house. He wondered how much of this Nadine had seen. None of it, he hoped, because priority one was getting her back on her feet. And, knowing her, recuperation would be stalled if she got to fretting about how she'd rebuild.

Oh, how he wanted to be with her now!

But Lamont knew in his heart what she'd ask of him, if she could: Stay, and explain things to her son and his family, and assure them that she'd be fine, right as rain, fit as a fiddle.

He'd teasingly called her the Mistress of Clichés at Lily's wedding reception. That memory conjured others, like the night they'd walked hand in hand around this very yard, and how she might have let him kiss her earlier, if Julie's helpful question hadn't interrupted, and—

"Here comes Nadine's boy," the EMT said, gesturing toward the pickup rolling up the driveway.

Lamont took a deep breath. Surely Adam had passed the ambulance, tearing the opposite way, as he headed for the farmhouse.

"Lamont," her son said, hefting his daughter from the car, "where's Mom?"

"She's on her way to Amarillo General. Just a precaution, I'm sure."

"Well, thank God for that," Adam said, staring at the smoking remains of the house.

"Do they know how it happened?"

Lamont turned toward the voice, and saw Julie, still sitting in the passenger seat, holding a paper napkin to her lips. "Sorry," he said, "but I can't tell you how it happened. Saw the flames from my place, called 911 on the way over." He didn't tell them the condition Nadine had been in when he'd found her, how pale and vulnerable she'd looked as the EMTs loaded her into the ambulance. Instead, he echoed the paramedic's words about her grit and stamina. With each syllable, Amy's blue eyes grew larger.

"If you hadn't shown up when you did, no telling—" Adam said again when Lamont finished.

"Mr. London," Amy interrupted, "did Grandmom get burnt?"

Honestly, he had no earthly idea. Everything happened so fast, he hadn't had a chance to check. Lamont tucked a stray blond curl behind her ear. "I don't think so, darlin'. She got a little smoke in her lungs, but the doctors at the hospital are going to fix her right up."

She put one tiny hand on either side of her father's face, exactly as Nadine had with Lamont earlier. "Will she die, Daddy?"

Adam's brow furrowed for a fleeing moment.

"'Course not," he said, forcing a grin. "You know Grandmom. Nothing can keep her down!"

When Amy looked to Lamont for confirmation, he nodded. "She'll be good as new and home again in no time."

"Can we go to the hop-sital, Daddy?" Amy asked. "I want to see her."

Adam swallowed, hard. "Well," he began, "I—"

"Tell you what," Lamont said. "It's late, and your grandmom had quite a night. She needs her rest. So how 'bout you and your mom and dad come on over to my house and try to get some shut-eye while your daddy checks up on Grandmom. And after a nice big breakfast tomorrow morning, we'll all go to the hospital together."

Her face brightened a bit. "Can we spend the night at Mr. London's house, Daddy? Can we?"

Adam exhaled a deep sigh. "Thanks, Lamont. That's mighty generous of you."

He waved the comment away. "Hey, what're friends for?" And, laughing, he added, "Besides, it'll be nice having y'all there. That place is way too big for one man."

Shoulders sagging, Adam heaved a heavy sigh and stared at what had been his childhood home. "Well, I guess there's nothing more we can do here."

"Meet you at River Valley," Lamont said. "If

you should get there before I do, the back door's unlocked." To Amy, he added, "Obnoxious is probably outside. He's gonna be one happy pup to have a little girl around to play with!"

Resting her head on her father's chest, she smiled sadly and nodded.

All the way back to the ranch, Adam's headlights danced in Lamont's rearview mirror. It dawned on him that Nadine, her son and his family had nowhere else to go. Would they accept his offer to stay at the ranch house until her own could be rebuilt? He wasn't at all sure, because Nadine could be mighty proud and stubborn when she put her mind to it.

Times had been hard for her these past few years, what with the drought and all. Now her house and everything in it was gone. The few pieces of furniture or clothing that hadn't burned to a crisp were too waterlogged from the fire hoses to be of any use. Maybe he could scare up something from one of his girls' boxes in the attic for her and Julie and Amy. His own clothes would be a tad big for Adam, but they'd do for the time being.

The welcoming golden glow of his ranch house came into view and, despite the horrible night, he managed a half grin, imagining Amy's tiny sneakered feet thumping up and down the hardwood stairs, giggling as Obnoxious ran close on her heels.

Sure would be nice having a little girl in the house again.

And in a few days, Nadine, big-eyed and gorgeous, would be smiling across the kitchen table at him. It would be even nicer having a *big* girl in the house again.

"I'm glad Adam decided to stay home and rest," Nadine said. "He was here all night."

Lamont nodded. "Julie is getting them settled in. Making breakfast. Unpacking the boxes of my girls' old clothes to see what might fit her." He chuckled. "She asked me to show her how to use the washing machine."

"I can't wait to get out of this place and plop myself into a chair at Kaye's salon. I guess that doesn't make much sense to you, though, does it?"

"No need to explain yourself to me," Lamont said, hands up like a robbery victim. "I understand. Completely."

Nadine shook a finger under his nose. "Don't give me that, cowboy. You don't understand diddly." She watched his dark brows move closer together.

He crossed both arms over his chest and, boots

shoulder-width apart, cocked his head. "You're mighty sure of yourself."

"I'd bet my house, if I still had one." She lifted her chin to hide the ache caused by stating the awful fact. "Because it's written all over your face."

Now the well-arched brows rose high on his forehead. "What's written all over my face?"

"You're confused. Bewildered—"

He closed one eye. "Mmm, wasn't that a song back in the '40s?"

Tempted to grin, she set her mouth in a taut line. She couldn't let him get away with changing the subject that easily. "You don't have a clue why I want to stop off at the beauty parlor on the way home."

"'Course I do." He tucked his fingertips into his jeans pockets. "You don't want your kids to see what the fire did to your hair, 'cause it might scare 'em."

Self-consciously, she put a hand on her flame-frizzed locks. He'd said it so matter-of-factly. And hit the nail square on the head, as her daddy used to say. Which shocked her, more than she cared to admit, because Ernest had never understood anything about her, least of all something as frivolous and vain as this. He'd have called the mission silly, a ridiculous waste of money.

Thankfully, Lamont broke the moment tension by making himself comfortable in the dusty-pink chair beside her hospital bed. "Soon as the nurse gives the nod, we'll head out. Need anything in the meantime?"

Closing her eyes, she bobbed her head left, then right, trying to flex kinked muscles. Evidently, she'd lain long enough in a pretzel position near the pantry to put a serious cramp in her neck. *Good old-fashioned massage would be nice,* she thought, rubbing her temples.

Nadine heard the shuffle of his boots on the fleck-tiled floor, then felt his big, warm hands on her shoulders. "Lamont London, what do you think you're—"

"Doc said you need some of this antibiotic ointment on your burns. Besides, looks to me like you could use a good old-fashioned rubdown. Between the concussion and everything else…"

Had she spoken her thoughts aloud? She must have; how else could he have known exactly what she'd been thinking?

Gently, he rubbed the healing salve into her knotted shoulder muscles. "Tell me if I get too rough," he said. "Sometimes, I don't know my own strength."

How many times had Ernest said *that?* Only every time he'd left her bloodied and bruised, which would amount to hundreds of times over their years together. For some reason she couldn't explain, Lamont's simple comment made her think of the time when she'd seen him lose his temper at the hardware store. His coupon was valid, he'd insisted, the sale on screwdrivers wouldn't officially end until closing. The gum-chewing teenager behind the counter relented, with one minute to spare, and Lamont filled it with a stern lecture about respect for one's elders and paying attention to details.

Suddenly, Nadine felt uncomfortable, having his hands on her, having him this close. Lamont must have sensed her tension, because he stepped back and gingerly wiped his oily palms on a tissue, plucked from the box on her bedside table.

She knew why he was being so careful with his hands, and felt horrible for comparing him to Ernest, especially when she could plainly see that the fire had turned his face sunburn red, how tiny pocks of the exploding windowpanes had dotted his cheeks, forearms and knuckles. He'd risked his life to save hers.

"Want me to check with the nurses' station?" he asked, tossing the tissue into the trash can. "See what's holding up your release?"

Unable to meet his eyes, Nadine shook her head. Once they left the hospital, there'd be the long ride home, and a stopover at the salon next door to Georgia's Diner. She needed to collect her thoughts, stiffen her resolve before spending that much time alone with Lamont. She'd made a promise to herself, and she aimed to keep it. She had no business entertaining romantic feelings for him because, fair or not, he too often reminded her of Ernest. She couldn't, *wouldn't* go back to hiding cuts and bruises, not even for the man who'd saved her life.

But wasn't she putting the cart before the horse? Because what made her think Lamont was interested in anything more than continuing their friendship?

Then she remembered the way he'd held her, how tenderly he'd looked at her after her party, just before Julie had called out. He would have kissed her, if not for the interruption.

That shouldn't change a thing. She was still the dirt-poor widow who'd just lost everything in a fire. He had a ranch of his own to run and surely he didn't need another burden to bear.

So why was he standing there, looking like a pup who'd just had his nose whacked with a rolled-up newspaper? He reminded her of Adam as a boy, when she'd said, "No cookies before dinner" or "You can't spend the night at Timmy's house." What stirred in her heart right now couldn't begin to compare with what she'd felt when her son wore that hangdog look. Moments ago, she'd accused Lamont of being confused when, in truth, it was *she* who had no explanation for the emotions warring within her.

Perhaps it was the concussion, or knowing she'd lost the house and everything in it, or the fact that Adam and Julie and Amy were homeless now, too, that made her want hide in Lamont's big, warm embrace, recapture the sensation of utter safety she'd felt when he'd held her after the fire. How strange it had been, feeling soothed by a man's hands after years of torture from Ernest's. Stranger still, feeling protected—even for a moment—in the arms of a man whose behavior occasionally raised ugly memories…

Had it been his deep, soothing voice, promising that everything would be all right, that started this battle between her sensible head and her romantic heart? Or that *way* he had of looking at her, reminding her that she was still a woman, despite having lived alone for years?

As he stared at the toes of his boots, the ceiling lights glinted from the silver strands peppering his dark hair. Nadine wondered if it would feel as think and soft as it looked.

He looked up just then and caught her staring. She tried…tried to pretend he wasn't standing there, boring into her with those long-lashed glittering gray eyes of his. Tried to ignore the captivating smile.

One thing was sure: It would be definitely be a long ride home.

Chapter Five

From her vantage point in the big mirror at Kaye Turner's salon, Nadine had a perfect view of Lamont. At first he'd paced near the wide window at the front of the shop. Now, a mini-traffic snarl outside captured his attention, and as he stopped to watch it, Nadine watched him. Something her Irish grandmother once said popped into her head. A year or so before the old woman died, she'd visited Nadine and, after being introduced to Lamont, fanned herself with a lacy hanky. "Ooo-eee!" she'd said. "Ye'd be smart not to let that one get away, Deenie. Why, he could star in a Hollywood movie, all tall, dark and handsome like he is." Winking, she'd added, "Yes indeedie, he's a…he's a fine fig're of a man!"

Thankfully, Lamont had been too far away to hear. "Gamma O'Riley, Sunday services are barely over!"

Winking one blue eye, she'd said, "God knows I'm right." She'd nodded toward the parking lot, where Lamont was climbing into his pickup. To this day, Nadine didn't know what made him look up just then, but he had, and when he'd waved, her heart did a little flip. "I might be an old woman, Deenie, but I know what I see, and that boy is moony-eyed for you."

Now, just as he had all those years ago, Lamont looked up again, this time meeting her eyes in the mirror. And, just as it had all those years ago, her heart did a little flip. *If anybody's moony-eyed,* she thought, pretending Kaye's movements had distracted her, *it's* me.

"You know I think the world of you," the stylist said, interrupting her reverie, "'cause I'd never open my shop on a Sunday for just anybody."

"You're a peach to do it."

"Well, when I heard about the fire and all, how could I *not?*"

Nadine patted the woman's red-taloned hand. "Thanks, Kaye. You're terrific."

"And so are you, kiddo."

He smirked. "This meeting of the mutual admiration society is now in session…"

Kaye clucked her tongue. "You're just jealous."

He chuckled. "Of what?"

She rested a fist on one plump hip, and pointed

at him with the rattail of her black plastic comb. "That you're not a member of the club."

His merry laugh echoed in the nearly empty shop. Nadine loved the sound of it, rich and full-bodied, starting somewhere deep in his chest and resonating upward.

"Only one who admires me is Obnoxious."

"That poor mutt," Kaye huffed. "Anybody named me 'Obnoxious,' I'd bite him." And without missing a beat, she pinched a few strands of Nadine's freshly shampooed hair between thumb and forefinger. "Mmm-mmm-mmm," she said, crimson lips pulled back in a teasing smile, "it'd be easier to shave you bald than try to clean up this mess."

"Which isn't out of the question," Lamont said, "considering who's wielding the shears." Another shrug. "But that's just my opinion."

He sat in one of the chairs under the window and began leafing through a fashion magazine. His body posture and facial expressions made it clear that he'd never set foot in a beauty parlor before. Still, he'd readily agreed to make the stop, and though Nadine suggested that he pass the time over a mug of coffee at Georgia's, he'd insisted on waiting for her here.

As Kaye's scissors flashed, Nadine tried to imagine a circumstance that would prompt Ernest to do something as kindhearted and understanding as this. When none came to mind, she sighed. And shrugged, unable to figure out why one minute she felt drawn to Lamont, the next, apprehensive.

"Nadine, honey, you're gonna look adorable with short hair," Kaye said as blond strands floated to the floor.

"Nadine, honey," Lamont echoed, "you'd look adorable bald."

Blinking, she looked into the mirror, hoping to get a glimpse of that same warm expression she'd seen moments ago. Unfortunately, Kaye blocked her view.

"If you think half-baked flattery will get you into the mutual admiration society," the hairdresser said, "you've got another think coming."

Nadine heard Lamont feign an exaggerated yawn as he went back to turning the pages of the magazine. Thankfully, Kaye's position hid the blush his compliment had caused. Since she couldn't thank the hairdresser out loud for unwittingly protecting her, Nadine decided to show her appreciation later with a generous tip.

But how could she do that when she didn't have a penny to her name? Her purse, with her wallet and checkbook inside, had gone up in flames, along with everything else in the house. Not that her bank book would've been much help, because she'd been running a zero balance for months. Not only couldn't she tip Kaye, she couldn't rent a place in town big enough for herself, Adam, Julie and Amy. What would become of her herd dogs and goats, and Julie's cat, Peepers?

Kaye's scissors click-clacked around her face, as bristly flaxen strands piled up on the polished linoleum. She closed her eyes, hoping the new shorter hairdo would be flattering. Her hair grew slowly and it had taken months to get it to shoulder length. Then, feeling like a feebleminded twit for even having such a vain thought amid all the mayhem, Nadine sighed again.

As the blow dryer hummed, she forced herself to think positive thoughts. Maybe things weren't as bad as they'd seemed, and she and the kids could live in the basement until repairs could be made. But even if that wasn't possible, and things were every bit as bad as they looked, the Lord would pull her through. He always had in the past.

"There y'go," Kaye said, spinning the chair to face the mirror. "What do you think?"

Nadine turned right, then left. She'd never worn her hair this short, but she'd get used to it. With God's help, she'd adjust to an apartment in the city and life without her critters, too.

"All the dead stuff's gone," Kaye added, ruffling Nadine's bouncy curls. "Nothing left but healthy, shining waves!" She whipped the pink smock from her client's shoulders. "You're gonna love having wash 'n' wear hair."

Good point, Nadine thought. With all she had to do in the next weeks, easy-care hair would be a blessing. "I'll have to pay you next time," she said. "My wallet was lost in the—"

"It's all taken care of, my dear." Kaye winked at Lamont, whose fire-reddened cheeks darkened with a blush.

In place of an explanation, he held open the door. "We'd better skedaddle if we want to get back in time to have supper with the kids."

Kaye draped a pearl-buttoned sweater over Nadine's shoulders. "Put this on," she said, shoving her friend toward Lamont.

Too much had happened in too short a time, and Nadine was having trouble taking it all in. Blinking back tears of gratitude and helplessness, Nadine said, "I'll return the sweater soon as—"

"Honey, don't you worry your pretty head about it. I have three more just like it upstairs." She gave Nadine a bear hug and bussed her cheek. "You need anything," Kaye said, holding her at arm's length, "anything at all, you call, hear?"

Nodding, Nadine followed Lamont to his pickup. They rode in silence for a few minutes before he reached across the seat to pat her hand. "Kaye was right."

"About?"

"You look adorable with short hair."

Her heart skipped a beat. A simple "thank you" would have sufficed. But she didn't want him comparing her to the women he'd so often joked with her about, who, in his words, "live and breathe to hear a man tell 'em they're purty."

"So do you," she said instead.

Both brows rose high on his forehead as Lamont met her gaze. "Uh, I, ah—"

The compliment rattled him, which only made him look more adorable. "I read a poll in a ladies' magazine once that said scars make a man look handsome."

Eyes on the road again, he huffed, shook his head. But she could see that he was grinning.

"Harrumph," he said, scrubbing a palm over his face. "If this mess turns into scars," he joked, "I might just give ol' Brad Pitt a run for his money."

She gave in to an urge and gently grazed his right cheek with her knuckles. "'Ol' Brad' only plays heroes in the movies, but you're a hero in real life."

Lamont swallowed, cleared his throat. "So… nice day we're having, don't you think?"

Yes, he was at least as uncomfortable with compliments as she'd always been. "Thank you,

Lamont," she blurted, "for pulling me out of the fire, and putting the kids up for the night, and picking me up at the hospital and—"

"It was my pleasure. All of it." He held up a hand to silence her. "I've had the feeling ever since we left the hospital that you wanted to ask me something." He glanced over at her. "And I'm pretty sure I know what it is."

"Is that so?" she asked, daring him to read her mind, yet again.

"You want to stop off at your place on the way to River Valley, have a look around."

Amazed, she nodded.

"That's okay with me, if you think you're up to it."

The question caught her off guard, and she bristled slightly. "'Course I'm up to it. Why wouldn't I be?"

"Well, the doc made it pretty clear. You're supposed to take it easy these next few days, because of the concussion and smoke inhalation."

As if on cue, she coughed. "Looking won't expend any energy." Unless, she thought, the sight was so horrible that—

"Isn't gonna be easy, looking at what's left."

No, she didn't suppose it would be. "I can take it. And if I can't, you'll be right there to rescue me."

He tucked in one corner of his mouth and

shrugged, and she took that to mean he didn't know what to make of her snappish tone. Nadine felt horrible, particularly considering all he'd done for her and the kids. "Sorry," she said, meaning it. "That was uncalled for."

"I'll just blame the headache."

She frowned. "How'd you know I have a headache?" The doctor had given her pain pills, but the throbbing hadn't started up in earnest until her head was hanging in Kaye's shampoo sink.

"I've taken a few whacks to the head in my day," he said, patting her hand, "so I know from personal experience that the so-called pain relievers the docs dole out don't come close to easing the pain." He grinned. "Don't worry, I won't hold your cantankerousness against you."

Before she could respond, he turned into her driveway. Almost immediately, the acrid scent of charred lumber assailed her nostrils. When the remains of the farmhouse came into view, she tried to stifle a gasp behind her hands. Nadine had seen the aftermath of house fires before, so what had she expected?

Certainly not this, Nadine thought. Certainly not nothing left at all.

Things had happened fast last night, too fast. As she'd fought to remain conscious, she hadn't been able to distinguish between flames and the strobes of emergency vehicles. Men shouted, but she hadn't understood a word. Only Lamont's voice, low and soothing, reached her: "Everything's gonna be okay, pretty lady. You're gonna be fine, I promise."

That bump on the head must have caused a disconnect between her brain and her mouth, because, hard as she'd tried, Nadine couldn't reassure him by saying, "Thanks" or "I know." The inability to communicate had scared her. Was it permanent? How would she read to Amy, or sing in the choir? To keep him from seeing fear in her eyes, she'd closed them. Well, that, and because during those moments in his arms, she'd read the concern on his face, and hadn't wanted to add to his worries. She remembered how cold and alone she'd felt, despite being surrounded by experienced paramedics. Remembered, too, how helpless and troubled he'd looked as they took her from his arms. Nadine remembered all that, but she didn't recall seeing the house ablaze.

Now, heart knocking against her ribs, she blinked back tears and held her breath. Thin wisps of smoke still spiraled from spongy, sooty ashes amid jagged black spikes—some no more than three feet tall—that had supported the walls and roof of her two-story home.

She opened the passenger door and stepped onto

grass, still wet from fire hoses. The doctor had said to expect headaches and light-headedness. He hadn't mentioned ringing in the ears, or the sweaty-yet-cold-all-over sensation that now prickled her skin.

Lamont's strong arm slid around her waist. How he'd reached her so quickly she didn't know, but Nadine said a little prayer of thanks. Had he pulled her close, or had dizziness made her lean into his hard, lean body? He stepped in front of her, gently gripped her biceps and, bending his knees, peered into her face. "You okay?"

"Yeah. Sorry."

Drawing her into a comforting hug, he kissed the top of her head. "Aw, darlin', whatever for?"

For behaving like a child, she thought. For getting weak-kneed and teary-eyed. Nadine pressed both palms against the soft fabric of his white shirt, then took a step back.

Nerves twitching, she plodded ahead, until she stood ankle-deep in the debris. Heat seeped through the soles of her shoes, even after all these hours and the hundreds of gallons of water that sogged the ashes. What could have caused a fire that burned so incredibly hot and fast?

Everything, it seemed, had turned to cinders—photographs, the Mothers' Day clay palmprint Adam had made in first grade, the framed copy of Amy's newborn footprint, her collection of wolf figurines, Gamma O'Riley's lace tablecloth, her mother's favorite soup tureen—gone, all gone.

She was about to turn away from the hideous sight when she stepped on something. "Oh no," she wailed quietly, digging it out. "It's Peeper's collar." There on her knees in the still-warm coals, she hugged it to her cheek. Was Julie's devoted feline gone, too?

"I'll bet she made it out alive," Lamont said, one big hand on her shoulder. "Cats are resourceful. Peeper could be anywhere, hiding until she thinks it's safe to come out."

"Maybe," she whispered. "I hope..."

In her prayer position, reality hit hard. Silent sobs shook her as she pressed the cat's collar to her chest. Peeper had spent every night of her five years in Amy's bed. The child would be heartbroken.

On his knees beside her, Lamont gathered her in his arms. "Shhh," he breathed into her hair, "don't give up hope just yet."

His kind, reassuring words, the comforting warmth of his strong arms around her, loosed a floodgate of hot tears.

"That's it," he whispered. "Get it all out now, so you can be strong for the kids."

If anyone knew how to handle grief and sadness,

it was Lamont. She'd seen him enough times with Rose to know that they shared far more than marriage and children. During their years together, they'd shared a love so deep and abiding that anyone who witnessed it felt humbled in its glow. Nodding, she patted his arm, a silent signal that her crying jag had ended.

As he helped her to her feet, a shard of sunlight glinted from something a few feet ahead. Nadine went toward it and, crouching, dug through the boggy dust again. "My father's pocket watch," she said, palming it, "minus the gold chain."

Standing, she rubbed away the grit and grime. The lid popped open, exposing old-fashioned numerals and filigreed hands. Amazingly, the thin second hand moved steadily clockwise in perfect rhythm with her heartbeat. "It was a wedding gift from my mother," she said, holding it out so Lamont could get a better look.

He didn't take it from her. Rather, he cradled her hands in his, leaned closer to read the inscription: "'I am my beloved's, and my beloved is mine.'" He met her eyes. "From the Song of Solomon."

Snapping the lid shut, she clasped it tightly in one hand. "I can't believe it survived all that heat," she said, mostly to herself.

"Good reason to believe Peeper survived it, too."

Maybe, she thought.

She didn't know how many minutes had passed as they stood side by side, staring at the scorched coals. Nadine wondered if, under similar circumstances, Ernest would have sensed that she required nothing more than his quiet presence to soothe her. Something told her that Lamont would have stayed with her forever, if he felt she needed it.

If she'd been keeping a ledger these past few months, with "Reasons to Like Lamont" in one column and "Reasons to Keep Your Distance" in another, Nadine knew which would be longer. Still, those few items on the Distance side troubled her, deeply.

Squaring her shoulders, Nadine took a deep breath. "Well, I guess there's nothing more we can do here. Might as well head on over to your house." She smiled up at him, hoping he hadn't seen her lips quiver. "Thanks for putting us up tonight. First thing tomorrow, I'll see about getting a place for the kids and me."

He led her back to the truck and gently closed the door. It wasn't until Lamont turned onto the highway that he said softly, "Nadine, I, ah, I didn't want to bother you with this before, what with all you're going through, but—"

"Lamont, you can tell me anything. You know that, don't you?"

"Yeah," he said, squeezing her hand. "But this is bad timing."

"No time like the present. Besides, I could use a distraction."

He turned on the radio. Turned it off again. "Peggy...Peggy quit on me."

"What? But she's been your housekeeper for—what—twenty years?"

He nodded. "I hired her full time about six months after Rose died."

"I don't get it. She always seemed more like a member of your family than an employee."

Lamont shrugged, as if to say he didn't get it, either. "Big place to maintain all by myself."

She pictured the luxurious ranch, with its looming ceilings, wide-planked floors, gourmet kitchen and grand staircase...

"I feel like a heel, asking you for a favor at a time like this, but...but I wonder if you'd consider taking her place." He held up a hand to silence her. "You and the kids are welcome to stay as long as you need to, in exchange for light housekeeping, and maybe you can fix supper once in a while. Temporarily, of course, until you rebuild and I find a new Peggy."

Move in with him—lock, stock and barrel? He must be joking.

One look at his somber expression made it clear: Lamont wasn't kidding.

"You'd have the whole upstairs to yourselves," he said, "My room is downstairs, way at the other end of the house. The biddies down at the beauty shop can't gossip, plus y'all would have as much privacy as you'd need. You'll hardly know I'm there."

He'd just proposed the perfect solution to her dilemma, so either she'd gone completely insane, or this was a dream. A beautiful, fairy-talelike dream. Because shouldn't she be the one saying, "You'll hardly know I'm there"?

"You'd be doing me a huge favor if you say yes."

What landlord in his right mind would rent them an apartment? She didn't have a penny to buy Amy a gumball, and neither did Adam, thanks to Julie's poor budgeting skills. Except for the kids' dime-store furniture, stored in the barn, they'd lost everything in the fire. So even if she found someone willing to trust her to come up with the money, how would they pay for food and utilities?

Nadine almost chuckled aloud, thinking that when the fire marshal finished his investigation, he'd blame the blaze on the mountain of bills stacked on her desk. The smile dimmed as she corrected herself: On what *had been* her desk.

"So…will you do it?"

If she said yes, she'd owe Lamont big-time, and not just dollars and cents. But if she said no, she and the kids would have to move into the local homeless shelter and get their meals at the soup kitchen. Her favorite Bible verse had always been 1 Corinthians 10:13, because the Lord had always known exactly how much bad news she could handle, and provided a way out. She believed He'd help her out of this predicament, too, but the way Nadine saw it, the price tag was enormous.

"Okay," she said slowly, "but only if you let me take Peggy's place. I want to do all the house-work—laundry, shopping, cooking, the whole nine yards."

"How 'bout we talk about it after your doctor gives you the green light. You suffered a concussion and smoke inhalation, don't forget. Besides, last thing I want is for you to feel like a—"

"—like a live-in housekeeper?" She laughed. "*If* I agree to this, that's the only way my con-science—and my ego—will allow it."

Nodding slowly, he exhaled a deep breath. "Okay. All right." He paused, but only for a second. "So what do you say? Will you help me out of this jam?"

The timing was just too perfect. And so was the situation. Working as his live-in housekeeper would keep the gossips' tongues from wagging, and keep her from feeling beholden. But no way she'd take the job if it meant putting a good woman out of work. "It just isn't like Peggy to leave you in a lurch this way. She must have given you a reason."

He swallowed, then cleared his throat. "She's been talking about taking an extended vacation for years, now. Said something about Hawaii."

Nadine remembered standing behind Peg at the convenience store recently. "Don't need to win millions," she'd said, waving her lottery ticket in the air, "just enough to take Ted to the islands for our anniversary." But if she'd won, Nadine would have heard about it at church, where the pastor and at least half of his flock saw the lottery as gambling, and therefore, sinful. The only other possibility that made sense was almost too awful to consider. "She's all right, isn't she?"

"Far as I know. Why?"

"I just can't figure out why she'd leave you after all these years." Then, "Her husband isn't ill, is he?"

"He's fine, too."

If that was true, then what was there to think about? Living and working at River Valley Ranch would put a roof over her kids' heads, and yet, she'd remain close enough to visit her own property every day, to feed and water her animals. There were phone calls to make and insurance forms to fill out. What better place to do it all than his house?

Like it or not, his suggestion made perfect sense. "All right, then. If you'll let me earn my keep, I'll do it."

"Excellent!" he said, beaming. "So, what's for supper, pretty lady?"

Pretty lady. It's what Ernest had always called her, while apologizing for beating her.

Please, Lord, she prayed as Lamont put the truck into Park, *don't let this be the biggest mistake of my life.*

Adam and his family greeted them at the front door. "Grandmom," Amy said, "wait until you see my room!" Blond pigtails bobbed as she jumped up and down. "Unka Lamont found clothes for me, too, up in his attic. He says they need warshin', though."

Chuckling, Adam mussed her bangs. "Sweetie, give her a minute to get inside before you drag her upstairs."

Forefinger to the tip of the child's nose, Nadine feigned a stuffy accent. "Yes, dah-ling, at least wait until the servants have carried all my valises up the grand staircase."

Giggling, Amy covered her mouth with a pudgy hand. "You sound just like a movie star." She hugged Nadine's legs. "You're funny!"

Adam frowned. "Honey, be gentle with Grandmom. She's bruised from head to toe, and—"

"It's all right," she said, returning the hug.

Despite her best efforts to hide her discomfort, Lamont saw it on her lovely face. He noticed that her gait didn't have its usual sprightliness, and neither did her usually musical voice. Dark circles had formed under her eyes, and her smile seemed practiced and tight. "Hey, Amy," he said, crouching, "how would you like some pizza for supper?"

Perching on his knee, she wrapped an arm around his neck. "Pizza? On a Sunday?" She looked to Julie for guidance. "Is that allowed, Mommy?"

"Sure," said her mother. "Why not?"

"Good," Lamont said, patting his stomach, "because I'm starving. And that's a problem, 'cause I have a lot in common with Old Mother Hubbard these days."

Amy slid from his knee. "You mean your cupboards are bare?"

"Not even a bone for poor old Obnoxious." He got to his feet. "So what do you guys like on your pizza?"

Amy began counting on dimpled fingers. "Pepperoni, mushrooms, sausage, green peppers, onions…but not olives." She wrinkled her nose. "'Specially not those yucky green ones. And cheese. Lots of cheese!"

Laughing, Lamont headed for the door. "Hey, Jules, how about calling in the order while I drive into town. That way, it'll be ready when I get there."

"Sure thing," Julie said, and disappeared into the kitchen.

Adam slid his wallet from his back pocket and held out a $20 bill.

But Lamont waved it away. "It's on me. We're celebrating tonight."

Before the younger man could protest, his little girl jumped up and down. "Celebrating?" Amy said, blue eyes shining. "Like a party?"

"Like a party," Lamont echoed.

As the child skipped off to join her mother, Nadine said, "Now, Lamont, we had a deal. I'm supposed to cook and—"

"Deal was," he interrupted, "you'd start all that after your doctor gives you the go-ahead."

When she smiled, he knew he'd won. This time, anyway. "Maybe while I'm gone, the kids can show you which room is yours." Half in, half out the door, he added, "Have a look in the closet. Lily says you're welcome to anything in there that fits."

Something between surprise and shame darkened her face, and before she had a chance to launch into an "I'm not a charity case" speech, Amy darted back into the room. "We're out of milk, Unka Lamont."

It tickled him that, already, the kid felt at home enough to say *we*.

"No bread or eggs in your 'frigerator, either."

He promised to get some on the way home, and closed the door behind him. Life would be a lot of things with Nadine and her family under his roof, he thought, grinning, but boring wouldn't be one of them.

As he drove toward Amarillo, he dialed his housekeeper's number. "Peg o' my heart," he said when she answered.

"Uh-oh…"

"Uh-oh?"

"Last time you called me that, you asked me to bake Cammi's wedding cake—two days before the wedding."

Chuckling, he said, "It's nothing like that, but I do have a favor to ask you."

"I'm rollin' up my sleeves as we speak…"

"I want you to take a vacation."

Silence, then, "A vacation?"

"Maybe you and that ornery husband of yours

can finally take that trip to Hawaii you've both been talking about for years."

"You call that *me* doin' *you* a favor?"

"Biggest I've ever asked of you."

Peggy sighed. Lamont could almost picture her, rosy-cheeked face crinkled in a confused frown as she fiddled with the coils of the phone cord.

"How long am I supposed to be on this *vacation?*"

It could take as long as a year to rebuild Nadine's house. "Six months, maybe more."

She gasped. "Good gravy, Lamont, you're not firing me, are you?"

"Of course not! You're terrific, and I honestly don't know what I would have done without you all these years."

"Okay. Out with it, bud. What's up?"

"I'm gonna level with you, but you have to promise not to breathe a word of this to anybody—especially Nadine—y'hear?"

"Got my oath hand in the air as we speak."

Lamont told her about the money troubles between Adam and Julie, and how they'd been forced to move in with Nadine, saving news of the fire for last. "She has nothing, Peg, and you know how proud she is. If I invited her and the kids to stay with me while they rebuild, she'd never go for it."

"I get it. She agreed if you'd let her do the housework in exchange for room and board."

"Bingo." Then, "Your lips are sealed, right?"

"Zipped," was her reply. "I won't even tell that ornery husband of mine. At least not until I've got him good'n buttered up with lotion on a sunny beach in Oahu."

"Thanks, Peg."

Her boisterous laugh punctuated his comment. "I don't know what you're thankin' *me* for, but you're welcome, boss."

"Just so Nadine won't get wise to the arrangement, how 'bout I pay you in advance, one big check to cover, say, six months' worth of salary?"

"Lamont London, you'll do no such thing! You've been more'n generous with me over the years. I know what other housekeepers get paid these days, and you've always given me double. So, thanks to you, I've managed to save up more than enough for a nice, long trip."

"But Peg—"

"No buts about it. I like Nadine, too. Remember when I threw my back out a couple years ago? Why, that li'l gal brought me casseroles three times a week, did my laundry and cleaned the place 'til it shined like a new penny! Let's say my absence is my contribution to the 'Get Nadine Back on Her Feet' fund."

He knew better than to argue with her, so tomorrow, he'd deposit a generous check in her bank account. "You're a doll, Peggy Flannigan. A living doll."

"You take real good care of our girl now, y'hear?"

"It'll be my pleasure," he said, and he meant it.

Chapter Six

Nadine leaned into the room and peered around slowly, thinking she could have fit her entire second floor into the space. The soles of her shoes sank into the plush carpet, silencing every cautious step. A shard of sunlight slanted across its deep burgundy border and illuminated bright white roses that bloomed in the center.

Nadine perched on the corner of the four-poster bed, absentmindedly fingering the clothes Lamont had neatly stacked on the silken coverlet. If she stayed here a year, she wouldn't have time to wear everything!

An antique mantel clock ticked steadily above the stone fireplace, reminding Nadine of her father's watch. Sliding it from her pocket, she popped the lid. Two minutes fast, she thought, grinning at its face. Snapping it shut again, she furrowed her brow, because the watch was about the only thing she could depend on right now.

Well, that, and Lamont.

His drive to Amarillo for pizza would keep him gone nearly an hour, more than enough time for her to shower and change into one of Lily's pretty outfits.

Nadine half ran downstairs to check on the kids, and smiled when she rounded the corner to the family room and found them cuddled together on the big leather sofa, fast asleep.

A quick inspection of the kitchen told her Lamont hadn't been exaggerating. The cupboards truly were bare. First thing tomorrow, she'd borrow his pickup and drive into town to restock the pantry. And the fridge and freezer, too. She'd never done anything halfway, and didn't intend to start now. After all he'd done for her and the kids, Lamont deserved her best.

She headed back upstairs and, closing the door behind her, rolled her eyes at the thought of calling this enormous, elegant room hers.

Lamont hadn't just laid out clothes for her, she realized. He'd provided everything a woman could possibly need—shampoo and conditioner, a hair dryer and curling iron, perfumed talc and a basket of assorted makeup products, still in their wrappers. They all seemed too new to have been Lily's.

Then she remembered that, after dropping her off at Kate's salon, he'd ducked out to run a few errands.

Behind the bathroom door, Nadine found a fuzzy white robe. On the hook beside it, blue pajamas, decorated with white moons and stars and, on the floor beneath it, matching slippers. Dense, oversized towels hung from the burled wood towel rack near the room-sized shower stall. After stepping out of her clothes, she grabbed one, then, twisted gleaming brass faucets, stood under the comforting spray.

Without warning, a steady stream of tears joined the warm water rushing down her cheeks. Was she crying because of all she'd lost? Or because, having lost everything, she'd become a charity case?

Suddenly, anger replaced sadness. "Lord," she whispered, eyes closed "give me strength like you've never given it before. Because I've never *needed* it more."

Lounging in his overstuffed leather recliner, Lamont remembered Nadine's "Norman Rockwell" comment. If the artist were still alive and working, Lamont would commission him to capture the scene before him.

Two pizza boxes lay open on the coffee table

between soda cans and a half-empty tumbler of milk. On her tummy in front of the armoire, Amy giggled at Shirley Temple, who mimicked a miniature monkey in a bellhop's uniform. Adam snored softly at one end of the sofa, and Julie dozed at the other, while Nadine pinched bits of crust between thumb and forefinger, and snuck them to Obnoxious.

Short bouncy blond curls framed her exquisite face, and not even baggy black sweatpants and a still-baggier T-shirt could hide her figure. After sneaking a last treat to Obnoxious, she folded her hands under her chin, and smiled at him. "What're you lookin' at, cowboy?"

You, he wanted to say, and who could blame him?

She pointed at the TV. "You're missing the best part."

Huffing, Lamont said, "Frankly, I wish the producers would shred every inch of that footage."

One hand over her chest, she gasped. "Lamont, this is an American classic!"

"Maybe so, but the networks air it so often, I'm sick of it."

"We are terrible, terrible people."

"Why?"

"Because I feel the same way!"

The only thing between them was a narrow end

table. He reached across it and grabbed her hand, giving it a gentle squeeze.

She eased her fingers from between his. "Think it's too warm for cocoa?"

"Cocoa!" Amy was on her feet in a flash. "My *fay*-vorite!" she squealed. "Can we have marshmallows on top, too?"

Nadine looked at Lamont. "Do you have any marshmallows?"

He rubbed his chin. "Don't rightly know." Fact was, he didn't know if he had the makings for cocoa, either, but he'd drive clear into town, right this minute, rather than disappoint Nadine or her adorable granddaughter.

He started to suggest that they all go to the kitchen to find out, but stopped himself. She'd feel a lot more at home if he let her rummage through the cupboards herself. "Why don't you two have a look-see? And if you don't find what you need, I'll drive us all into Amarillo for the supplies. I need to restock the pantry, anyway."

Nadine's warm smile was proof enough that he'd made the right choice. He watched her pad out of the room, fuzzy slippers flip-flopping against the soles in sync with the tick-tack of Obnoxious's claws on the hardwood. He knew it was selfish, but Lamont hoped it would take months, years even, to settle her insurance claim, interview contractors and rebuild. Because what he'd told her earlier had only been half true.

He would enjoy having her here, and already regretted the day she'd have to move into a place of her own.

Chapter Seven

Amy looked so sweet in her frilly fairy princess dress and matching pink tiara that Lamont could barely resist the urge to hug her. He hadn't felt this content in the big old house since his own girls were small. Her happy laughter and innocent games were proof that in the weeks she'd been at River Valley, Amy felt more and more like it was home. Maybe too much at home, if the mess on his office floor was any indicator.

"Young lady," he said as she skipped into his office, "we need to have a talk."

The instant she saw him kneeling amid the clutter, her playful smile vanished, and before he had a chance to ask what had happened, tears pooled in her big blue eyes. "I didn't mean to do it," she said. "It was a ax-dent."

Sitting in his high-backed desk chair, he plucked

a tissue from the container between his boots and patted his thigh.

Head down, she took slow, careful baby steps toward his outstretched arms.

"Now then," he said, settling her on his knee, "how 'bout telling me what happened in here?"

She let him blot her tears, then said, "I was looking for crayons, and thought maybe you keep them up there." Amy pointed at a high shelf on the bookcase behind him. "I couldn't reach, so…"

So she'd pulled out the file drawers, and used them as steps, Lamont reasoned. And the cabinet tipped, spewing papers like a metal Vesuvius. "Darlin'," he said, gently holding her upper arms, "do you realize how dangerous that was? Why, that cabinet could have landed on top of you and…" The horrible image cut his words short, and he gave her a little shake, as if to punctuate his fear.

"Oh, Unka Lamont." Sniffling, Amy buried her face in the crook of his neck. "Please don't be mad at me."

Gathering her close, Lamont kissed the top of her head. "Aw, I'm not mad." He held her at arm's length. "I am a little disappointed, though. Do you know why?"

"'Cause I came in here without permission?"

Resisting the urge to grin, he chucked her chin. "That's right. Now, next time you can't find something, I want you to come find me, and we'll look for it together. Okay?"

Wiping her nose on a ruffled pink sleeve, she nodded.

"Now what do *you* think your punishment should be…for breaking the rule?" *And for scarin' the daylights outta me.*

On the heels of a deep sigh, Amy's brow furrowed as she considered possible consequences for her actions. "No dessert for a year, and no Shirley Temple movies for *two* years."

Smiling, Lamont pressed a fingertip to her lips. "I don't think we need to do anything that—"

"Mean?" she finished.

Smiling, Lamont said, "It isn't 'mean' for someone who loves and cares about you to do whatever it takes to keep you safe." Hands bracketing her cherubic face, he forced a frown. "I don't make up these rules just for the fun of it, you know. There's a good reason for them." A silvery tear tracked down her cheek, and he caught it with the pad of one thumb.

"All right," she said, shoulders slumped. "Let me have it. What's my punershment?"

Lamont scratched his chin and narrowed one eye. "I think, for something like this, fifteen minutes in a chair is perfect."

Her eyes brightened. "Thanks, Unka Lamont!"

Hugging her tight, he laughed and, kissing her cheek, said, "Which chair will you sit in?"

"Oh, that's easy," she said, smiling. "Yours, of course."

"Why that one?"

"'Cause it smells like you, and I love how you smell!" She climbed from his lap and headed for the door. "Will you tell me when my time is up, so I can help you clean up this big mess?"

"That's okay, kiddo. I'll take care of it."

She disappeared around the corner, reappeared even before he'd bent to retrieve the first file folder. "Can I read while I'm punished?"

"Sure." Amy was halfway down the hall when he added, "Just make sure it's a book you can reach without climbing!"

Ten minutes later, he found her in the family room, curled up in his chair, leafing through a gigantic picture book. He perched on the arm and said, "Good news, time's up."

Amy's brow furrowed as she closed the book. "Already?"

"Already," he said, ruffling her hair. "Now what say you have some fun on the tire swing?"

Blond curls bobbing, Amy got to her knees and wrapped her arms around him. "I love you, Unka Lamont."

"Love you, too, darlin'." Surprised by the tears

stinging his eyes, Lamont quickly added, "I'm hungry. How 'bout a snack before you head outside?" And before she could answer, he scooped her up and carried her into the kitchen. "I'm in the mood for a fried egg sandwich."

"Me, too." Hiding a grin behind one hand, she added, "Can I have bacon on mine? I *love* the way you fry bacon."

Hours later, Lamont decided to fix the loose hinge on the back door, and took a shortcut through the family room. Amy sat in his chair, quietly scribbling in a coloring book, while her dad slept soundly on the sofa.

"You must've spiked a fever," he said, nudging the younger man's boot with his own, "or you'd be in the barn, ankle-deep in hay."

"Oh. Sorry." Adam sat up and rubbed his eyes. "Just sat down minute, to think a spell. Guess I must've dozed off."

"Guess you can't walk and chew gum, either."

"Huh?"

Lamont shook his head. "Can't think and work at the same time?"

The younger man frowned. And so did Lamont. "Best way I've found to deal with your troubles," he said, "is to bury 'em. Bury 'em deep under hard, backbreaking work. That's how I got through those first miserable months after…" Even after all these years, he couldn't make himself put *Rose* and *died* in the same sentence. "…after I lost Rose."

Shoulders slumped, Adam nodded. "I'll try, but—"

"Ever see *Star Wars?*"

Adam frowned.

"That old wrinkled dude—I forget his name—said something my own pa used to tell me when I was a boy, 'Do or do not. There is no *try.*' That's good, solid advice, and you'd be wise to take it."

Lamont went off to fix the hinge and repair the doorknob, too, when he heard Adam in the barn, tossing things around and grumbling like a grizzly with a toothache. Lamont tried to put himself in the boy's shoes. If his wife had emptied their bank accounts and gotten them evicted, he'd have been just as angry. Would've felt betrayed and hurt, to boot.

Yet another reason to thank God for his years with Rose. To his knowledge, she'd never kept a secret from him. Always frugal, even in good times, the woman could stretch a dollar to the snapping point, and do it without a word of complaint. If Julie didn't even possess enough confidence in Adam to confess checkbook errors, where would she find the fortitude to make things right down at the bank—and between her and her husband!

He'd heard it said that girls often marry men

like their dads. Too bad the reverse wasn't true, because Adam would have been a good sight better off if he'd picked a girl more like his mother.

Instantly, Nadine's image popped into his head. Thank the good Lord, he thought, that he was alone on the porch, because he'd have a dickens of a time trying to explain why oiling a squeaky hinge made him grin like the Cheshire cat.

Nadine dragged the vacuum cleaner into the family room. "I thought your daddy was asleep in here," she said, kissing Amy's forehead.

The child turned a page in her book. "He woked up when Unka Lamont yelled at him."

She put down her dust cloth. Lamont had scolded her son? "What're you doing inside on such a pretty day?"

"Well, at first it was 'cause Unka Lamont told me to sit here. And now, it's 'cause I *want* to."

"Why did he tell you to sit here?"

"'Cause I made a big mess in his office."

"You did?"

The child never looked up from her work. "Uh-huh."

But she'd just been in his office, and hadn't noticed so much as a paper clip out of place. Her heart ached for Amy, far too young to understand why her family had been traipsing from place to place like a band of nomads these past few months, or why her parents couldn't spent two minutes in the same room without arguments and accusations. Despite it all, Amy's sunny disposition had remained intact—during daylight hours, anyway. Fitful sleep and frequent nightmares were proof that the situation was taking a toll on her.

Lamont had raised four girls, so why couldn't he see that?

Yes, it had been an incredible act of Christian kindness, the way he'd welcomed them into his home. Nadine owed him a lot, and so did her kids. She'd kept her end of the bargain, after all, cleaning and cooking, taking care not to overstep her bounds. Maybe it was time to suggest that the next time he was tempted to browbeat her son or discipline her granddaughter, he talk it over with her first.

"I'm going to see if your daddy would like some lemonade. Would you like some, too?"

Peeking over the pages of her book, Amy's eyes crinkled with a sweet grin. Oh, how she loved this child!

"Can I have chocolate milk instead?"

"Of course you can." Nadine kissed the top of her head. "I'll be back in just a few minutes, with chocolate milk *and* cookies!"

She found Adam in the barn, shoveling dung

from the horse stalls. "What happened to your plan to take a short nap?"

Without looking up, he said, "Seems your boyfriend had other plans."

"First of all," she said, "he is *not* my boyfriend. And second, I want to know what, exactly, he said to set you off."

Adam draped gloved hands over the pitchfork's handle and shook his head. "It seems he sees me as some kind of knock-kneed sissy, wallowing in self-pity because Julie's stupidity put us in the poorhouse."

"Adam," she said, "there's no need to resort to name calling."

He gave a shrug and got back to work. "Maybe Lamont has a point. Beggars can't be choosers, after all."

Nadine felt her cheeks reddening. Was that really how Adam saw things? "Honey," she began carefully, "I'll agree that between the fire and Julie's lack of bookkeeping skills, you have a lot on your mind. But living here…well, I'd hardly call us beggars. We all pull our fair share of the load around here. Why, even Amy makes her bed and picks up her toys every day."

If he heard her, Adam gave no sign of it. So she grabbed his right hand and yanked off his glove.

"Just look at those blisters. You didn't get them lounging around, wallowing in self-pity!"

Adam pressed a light kiss onto Nadine's cheek, then took back his glove. "I hate to admit it, but I never broke a sweat to earn 'em, either." Grinning mischievously, he waved her away. "Now get on back to your woman's work, why don't you, so I can rub another callus onto my manly palms."

It had been a long time since she'd seen him smile that way. God bless him for trying to make the best of a bad situation. "You're not too old to turn over my knee, y'know," she teased. "By the way, where's Lamont?"

"Uh-oh, I know that look. You aimed it at me every time I messed up as a kid. Do me a favor, Mom, and let *me* decide whether or not I need defending."

"Are you aware that he punished Amy?"

Again, he leaned on the tool. "For what?"

She shook her head. "She said something about making a mess in his office."

"You know as well as I do that he pretty much gave us the run of the place. The only room that's off-limits is his office. Amy knows that, so if she went in there—and I don't see why Lamont would give her a time-out if she didn't—then she needs to pay the price." He met her unwavering gaze with one of his own. "Isn't that how you taught *me* to respect the privacy and property of others?"

"Well, yes, I suppose. But I didn't see evidence that she'd—"

"What *I* see is that no amount of work we do around here can repay him for what he's doing for us. The least we can do is show the man a little respect, and stay out of the one room he's asked us to stay out of."

He wasn't her little boy anymore, that was for sure. And he was right, too. "How 'bout if I make your favorite for supper—spaghetti and meatballs with garlic bread, and tapioca pudding for dessert?"

"Sounds great."

As she made her way out of the barn, he said under his breath, "Things could be worse, you know. Lots worse. We could have our present difficulties, and Pa to cope with."

A chill snaked up her spine at the mere thought of it. And the main reason she managed to shake it off so quickly was because of Lamont's generosity. "Have I told you lately how proud I am of the man you've become?"

Chuckling, Adam shook his head and went back to work. "Call me when it's time to lick the tapioca spoon."

Head down, Nadine hurried along the flagstone

path connecting the barn to the kitchen, thanking the good Lord for closing the book on the Ernest chapter of their lives. Adam had been right. If they'd been forced to cope with his father's ferocious temper on top of everything else—

"Ooomph," Lamont sputtered as wrenches, pliers and screwdrivers clanked to the walk. Grinning, he worked his jaw from side to side. "Where are you going in such an all-fired hurry?"

"Sorry," she admitted, touching the tender spot where his chin and her forehead had collided. "I didn't see you." She realized suddenly that she'd forgotten to ask if Adam might like some lemonade. "I was just going inside to start supper."

Laughing, Lamont bent to collect his tools. "Supper? But it isn't even lunchtime yet, pretty lady."

Oh, how she wished he'd quit calling her that, because it was almost word for word what Ernest said to her after a beating. It made her wince. "The sauce needs hours and hours to simmer," she explained, stooping to help him gather nails and nuts. Nadine was happy to have the distraction, because with the uncomfortable subject of Adam's scolding and Amy's punishment between them, she didn't trust herself to meet his eyes.

"What's on the menu?"

"Spaghetti," she said. And as she leaned forward

to collect a runaway bolt, Nadine's forehead plowed into Lamont's chin a second time, this time knocking him off balance. Lying on his side in the fetal position, he started to laugh, a low rumbling sound that built in volume and heartiness.

When or how it happened, Nadine couldn't say, but she found herself wrapped in his powerful arms. Soon, the merriment subsided, and in the ensuing silence, her pulse pounded with anticipation…and dread.

One big hand behind her head, Lamont drew her closer, and when he spoke, his deep voice trembled slightly. "Ahh, Nadine, for such a delicate li'l thing, you sure do have a rock-hard head."

Chapter Eight

On the night of the fire, the insurance adjuster came very close to blatantly accusing her of setting fire to her own house, and during those first weeks she and the kids had been with Lamont, Nadine prayed daily that the police and fire marshal would conclude it had been a horrible accident, because without that check, she'd lose everything. And she'd said the same prayer every morning and every night since.

When the doorbell rang and she saw Marcus Templeton on the front porch, her heart hammered. "Please, God," she prayed as she unbolted the door, "let him have come to deliver good news...."

His height and breadth nearly filled the doorway, blocking most of the sunlight from the usually bright foyer. Waving him inside, she smiled. "Good to see you, Marcus. Please, come on in."

It felt more than a little odd, welcoming a visitor into Lamont's home, as if she'd become the lady of the house. The idea died a quick death as two long strides put Templeton smack in the middle of the entry, where he stood, booted feet shoulder width apart, tapping a packet of official-looking papers against his meaty thigh.

"How's Marta?" she asked. "I heard she's been under the weather."

Templeton's smoke-raspy interruption echoed in the entryway. "She's fine," he barked. Then, as if regretting his gruff response, he cleared his throat. "It was just the flu, but you know Marta. Everything's a big production." Inhaling deeply, he held out the papers. "'Fraid it's official business that brings me here this mornin', Nadine."

Every nerve twitched as she accepted the blue-sheathed package. "What is it?"

"Summons."

She blinked up at him, wishing Lamont would get back from town. He would sure be a comfort right about now. "But…whatever for?"

Marcus's thick mustache slanted above a "You must be joking" smirk. "Look, Nadine, we go back a long way, so I ain't gonna beat around the bush."

She made no attempt to mask her annoyance. "Good, because that'd be a colossal waste of time, and unnecessarily hard on the shrubbery."

One bushy brow rose as he contemplated her remark. Then he said, "You can't be surprised to hear that you're the only suspect in the house fire."

Nadine held her breath. A suspect? How had he come up with such a crazy notion?

"My investigation is purt-near complete," he continued, "and—"

"Marcus," Lamont said, sidling up beside Nadine.

She'd never been so happy to see anyone in her life. Despite decades of single-handedly running her ranch—with reasonable success, until the past few years—she'd never perfected Lamont's ease with the likes of Marcus Templeton.

"What brings you all the way out here?" he asked, right hand extended in greeting.

The man nodded at the papers Nadine held. "I'll need her to come to town, soon as possible."

She took a step toward the growling bear of a man. "Why?"

"Some things I'd like to ask you, some things I'd like you to look at," he offered, "startin' with the insurance investigator's report."

"Can't we take care of that here?"

He shook his head. "Nope. It's procedure. Any statement you make has to be a matter of record, or it won't hold up in court."

"Court?" Nadine's heart rate doubled.

Before Marcus could explain, a Potter County squad car pulled into the circular drive. No one spoke as Sheriff Hayden Wallace slid from behind the wheel, hitching up his trousers as he climbed the porch steps toward the still-open door. "Mornin', folks."

"Glad you could make it," Marcus said.

At first sight of the documents in Nadine's hands, Wallace winced apologetically. "I see you already got the bad news."

Lamont relieved her of the papers and, unfolding them, began reading.

"I don't understand," Nadine said. "At the hospital that night, you said—"

"I said we were finished, for the time being. I never meant to imply that the investigation was complete." He shrugged one burly shoulder and launched into a recitation of his scientific facts.

Nadine, straining to pay attention, massaged her temples. A nightmare had awakened Amy, who'd spent the remaining hours in the security of her grandmother's arms. Unfortunately, providing that comfort proved costly to Nadine, whose fitful sleep was peppered with dreams of Ernest and fire and the tension between Adam and Julie.

She'd prepared a hearty breakfast and lunch for the rest of the household, but hadn't felt much like eating, herself. Nadine blamed sleep deprivation and hunger for the thrumming, hissing sounds pounding in her ears.

"…point of origin…accelerant…source of ignition…flashpoint…"

His voice faded in and out, as if someone was slowly rotating the volume dial on a car radio on, then off again. As the hulking bodies of the three men in the foyer became shadowy, undulating shapes, a dizzying yellow haze veiled her world. She'd never fainted—not once in her life—but something told Nadine that's exactly what was about to happen, right here, right now. Though she gulped air to prevent it, her body went weak and her knees buckled. Odd, she thought, puddling to the floor, how like a marionette she felt, one whose puppeteer had let go of the strings. The icy marble felt good against her clammy cheek, and she gratefully closed her eyes…

"Nadine? Nadine, look at me. Open your eyes, darlin'…"

Despite the fog shrouding her mind, she recognized Lamont. Recognized, too, the same troubled tones that had tinged his otherwise honeyed voice on the night of the fire.

After he'd risked his life to save her own.

While she lay limp and nearly unconscious in his strong arms.

And the sirens wailed closer, closer.

As paramedics took her from his caring embrace.

What a peculiar dream this was, where her thoughts surged from how peaceful and calm Lamont's life had been, until that night, until she and her family invaded his home and his world, to the realization that she should've listened to her better instincts, taken an apartment in town, sold some few acres to finance the rebuilding and tide them over until they were back on their feet.

But she couldn't go back in time. Couldn't undo what she'd done to him.

His voice reached her again, soothing, comforting, reassuring. "I'm fine," she tried to say. But her brain and her tongue refused to cooperate. Maybe the truth was she wasn't fine. How could she be, with the authorities convinced that she'd burned down her own house? Worse, she had no one but herself to blame. *You'll find a way,* she'd repeated to herself, month after month when the bills came due and the money to pay them didn't materialize. *You always do.* Stubborn pride kept her from turning to God. Too late now to expect the Lord to answer her prayers.

Shame replaced guilt, remorse took the place of regret. This was no time for self-pity. She needed to get back on her feet, fight to prove her innocence.

"That's it, sweetie," Lamont was saying, "look at me."

He cupped her chin in one powerful hand, held her upper body close to his, so close she could feel the hard beating of his heart. His big, generous heart.

"Get her a glass of water," she heard him say before heavy footsteps hurried down the long hall. Lamont's big fingers combed back her bangs, stroked her cheeks while cabinet doors opened and closed in the kitchen. Which one of the important, uniformed men, she wondered, had obeyed his water-fetching orders? Only a man like Lamont London could evoke such immediate obedience from men of authority.

She heard running water, the return of booted feet as Lamont helped her sit up, tasted cool water as it touched her lips. "Thanks," she said, meeting his worried eyes.

"Ah, darlin'," he said, pulling her closer, "you sure do know how to scare a fella."

Hayden got onto one knee beside them and removed his Stetson. "You okay, Nadine?"

Nodding, she scrambled to her feet. "Yeah, I'm fine." Steadying herself on the foyer table, she said, "Guess that'll teach me to skip meals."

"I still need you to come down to the office," said Marcus.

"Marcus," Hayden barked, "at least give her a minute to get her sea legs, why don't you?" He sent her a friendly wink. "You've known this li'l gal all her life. If she says she'll be there, you can count on it."

Marcus shrugged again. "Desperate people do desperate things."

Nadine took a deep breath, let it out slowly before saying, "I'll grant you, Marcus, these are pretty dire circumstances." Lifting her chin a notch, she said, "Name the day and time."

He glanced at his watch. "Three o'clock?"

"Today?" Lamont asked, his voice reflecting both shock and disdain. "But that barely gives her time to—"

"I'd just as soon get it over with."

"Then I'm coming, too."

Amy skipped into the foyer, a grinning Obnoxious on her heels.

"We'll need to find Julie or Adam," Nadine whispered, "let them know we'll be gone for a few hours."

"Where you goin', Grandmom? Can I come, too?"

She squatted and gathered her granddaughter in a loving hug. "Not this time, sweetie pie. I have some important—" she bit her lower lip to still its trembling "—some business to take care of in town, and you'd be bored silly." Holding Amy at arm's length, she winked. "If you're a good girl while Lamont and I are gone, I'll make your favorite for dessert."

Clapping, Amy giggled. "Oh, goody! A hot fudge sundae?"

"With double fudge."

Satisfied, Amy hop-skipped all the way to the top step, where her mother scooped her up. For an instant, the younger woman's gaze held Nadine's. Standing, Nadine summoned courage she didn't feel. "I don't want you kids to worry, okay? Everything's going to be fine." Julie's anxious smile wavered slightly before she ducked out of sight.

The peck of dog claws on the marble floor drew Nadine's focus back to the foyer, where Lamont closed the door none too gently behind Marcus and Hayden. A frown furrowed his brow as he glanced toward the top step. Was he, like Nadine, wondering why Julie had appeared and disappeared so quickly?

He shrugged and shook his head, then took Nadine's hand and led her into the kitchen. He pulled out a chair and pointed at its red-and-white-checked seat. "Don't you move from there, young lady, until I get some vittles into your belly. How's fried eggs and bacon sound?"

She nodded. "Sounds great." But her growling

stomach was the least of her worries. A glance at the clock told her that in a few hours, she might take her next meal behind bars. She was so lost in thought that when Lamont put a steaming mug of coffee in front of her, Nadine lurched.

He gave her hand an affectionate squeeze. "Remember what you told Julie earlier?"

That everything would be fine? Right, Nadine thought with a harrumph.

"Well, it's true," Lamont said.

She smiled past hot tears that stung her eyes. "From your lips to God's ear."

Nadine didn't think she'd ever spoken the words with more fervor.

The meeting didn't go well. Not well at all. If somebody didn't present the cops with tangible proof of Nadine's innocence...

Lamont didn't want to think about what could happen to her.

They had an hour or so before supper, so he suggested that Nadine spend it napping with Amy and much to his surprise—and relief—she went without argument.

Locked in his office, he rifled through his Rolodex, searching for a number he hadn't called in years. His college roommate had invested twenty years with the Big Apple's homicide division before an on-the-job injury forced his early retirement. Never one to let life pass him by, Frank Duvall had come home to Texas and opened a one-man private investigation service.

"D and D Investigations."

"Well, as I live and breathe, if it isn't Lanky Frankie, himself."

"Lamont London, you ol' hoot-owl you. How long has it been?"

It had always amazed him that such a booming voice could resonate from such a slender frame. "Too long," he said, chuckling.

"So how are ya, pal o' mine?" Frank said.

"Good, good. How 'bout you? Still a confirmed bachelor?"

The familiar grating laugh wafted into Lamont's ear. "Is the '65 Corvette still the best car on wheels?"

Back in college, Frank had inherited a couple thousand dollars from his grandfather's estate, and spent every dime overhauling a beat-up 'Vette. "Don't tell me you're still drivin' that bucket of bolts."

"Just put a new convertible top on 'er, as a matter of fact." A second ticked silently by before he said, "But something tells me you didn't call to talk about my 'baby.'"

"If you can meet me for breakfast tomorrow, I'll tell you all about why I called."

What a relief it was to walk into the family room and see Lamont reading the paper. "You're up way past your bedtime," Nadine said, plopping onto the corner of the sofa nearest his chair.

"Couldn't sleep." He folded the newspaper, and tossed it onto the coffee table.

She rubbed her eyes. "Me, either. I'll probably see those photographs in my mind's eye until I draw my last breath."

Eight-by-ten color photos of the fire's aftermath seemed etched to the insides of her eyelids. After studying the height of smoke patterns on what remained of her walls and looking at eerie, ghostly shapes forever burned into the floorboards, Marcus had determined that the fire had been set deliberately. "Funny," she said, "but I didn't notice gasoline and kerosene when we were at the house. Didn't Marcus say it was the first thing he detected once he got on the scene?"

"Yeah, but you'd inhaled buckets of smoke, darlin'. No way your sniffer was working properly that morning."

Yes, that could very well explain why she hadn't smelled—what had Marcus called them?—accelerants.

He reached across the end table and grabbed

her hand. "Why didn't you tell me you were in so much trouble?"

"Shame. Embarrassment." She shrugged. "I'm still not sure how things got so far out of control. I've been managing the Greeneland books since long before Ernest died, so I should have seen the signs." She sighed. "Guess I didn't want to face the obvious, and do what had to be done."

"Such as?"

"Could've sold some of the land, for starters."

Lamont harrumphed. "Right. So some greedy developer could move in and gobble up the territory, acre by acre?"

"I can see the headline now," she said, drawing quote marks in the air, "'Nadine Greene, Public Enemy Number One.'" Another sigh. "Ironic, isn't it, that I ended up there, anyway?"

"Nobody sees you that way—least of all me." Then, "Why didn't you come to me?"

"What, so you could saddle your white steed, come riding to my rescue? Again?" A bitter laugh escaped her throat. "Neither my bank account nor my ego could've survived that."

She watched him stare ahead in stony silence, saw his eyes and lips narrow. "First, you don't know me half as well as you think you do. Second, I have way too much respect for you to just fork over a pile of cash, like you're some spoiled brat who spent all her allowance on lipstick and fingernail polish. We could have worked out a way for me to help, a way you wouldn't have viewed as ego-damaging." Frustrated, he enclosed the fingers in a loose fist and blew a puff of air through his teeth. "If we'd talked about it, that is."

She owed him a lot. Probably wouldn't live long enough to repay his many kindnesses. But if he expected her to apologize for wanting to solve her problems, he was in for a long wait.

"You're the most stubborn woman I've ever known." He took back his hand. "And it's downright arrogant the way you decided how I'd react if you came to me for help."

He had a point. Sort of. A sense of helplessness washed over her. If her life had ever felt more out of control, she couldn't say when. Why, she couldn't even figure out how to apologize for hurting his feelings.

"So, you're gonna pout now, are you?"

That got her attention. "Excuse me?"

"It hasn't escaped my notice that every time I say something you don't want to hear," he growled, "you dish up a healthy portion of the silent treatment."

This was how Ernest started every beating: First, he'd invent some half-baked excuse to lob accusations, hurling insults until he'd built up a head of steam that granted him self-appointed permission to thrash the stuffing out of her. Eventually, too tired to throw any more punches, he threw excuses, instead, if she hadn't said this or done that, he never would have lost control. And in a day or two, when the welts and bruises looked their worst, he'd shower her with flowers and candy and "I'm sorry, pretty lady" apologies.

"If I didn't know better," she muttered, "I'd say you and Ernest were blood kin."

Much as he would have liked to ask what *that* meant, Lamont held his tongue. Yeah, it hurt, knowing she hadn't come to him when things got bad. But, then, she'd been on her own for so long that she'd probably forgotten *how* to ask for help. He felt like a first class heel—if heels came in classes—for not showing her more understanding and compassion.

He reached for her hand again and this time she flinched. "Hey, look," he began, "don't pay me any mind, okay? If I came off sounding like a bully…" No *if* about it, her stony expression told him, and the truth of it shamed him to the soles of his boots. "I'm sorry, pretty lady. Honest."

She shrugged one shoulder. "What's done is done."

Now he had *two* reasons to feel like a heel. In years past, it had crossed his mind a time or two that things weren't exactly peaceful in the Greene house. Wearing long sleeves and trousers, even in the blistering Texas heat, not showing up when she'd promised to help out with church socials, the nervous smile that never quite reached her eyes whenever he saw her with Ernest. Why had he allowed thoughts like "It's nobody's business" to overpower "You know the right thing to do"? Furious with himself, Lamont thumped the arm of his chair, making her lurch, and making *him* more sure than ever that she had, indeed, been abused.

But what to do about it now?

From out of nowhere, a memory flashed in his mind, of Rose, who'd come home after a writing class glowing with pride because her instructor had written, "You've mastered 'Show, don't tell!'" on the first page of her short story. And it wasn't just good advice for authors.

Nothing he could say could make up for past negligence or insensitive words already spoken. There were, however, things he could *do*.

And he'd do them, or die trying.

He'd avoided her all day, and it was just as well, because Nadine didn't think she'd know what to say, even if she *could* meet his eyes. Last night, after she'd said goodnight—and he hadn't responded—she'd spent hours praying for forgiveness. What sort of woman makes a man feel ill at ease and unwelcome in his own home? Especially after he'd willingly opened it to her and her kids?

Thankfully, Amy's nonstop chatter helped ease things during supper, giving her time to try to figure out how to make it up to him. It wasn't his fault, after all, that some of the things he said and did reminded her of Ernest. And it wasn't fair, either, to equate his matter-of-fact way of talking with her husband's violent tendencies.

One by one, she slid plates into the dishwasher's lower rack and filled the top with glasses and cups. She set aside the pots and pans, grabbed the carving knife, intending to add it to the hand-wash pile. Her own scowling reflection in its gleaming blade brought back the frightening memory of the time Ernest chased her around the kitchen with one just like it. If he hadn't missed, snapping the blade as it hacked into the doorframe…

A shudder passed through her, and she dropped the knife into the dishpan. Somehow, she couldn't imagine Lamont going at Rose with a knife. Or his fists. Or an open hand, she thought, reaching into the sudsy water to retrieve it.

"You still in here all by your lonesome?"

Startled, Nadine did an in-place two-step. "Julie, I declare," she gasped, pressing a palm to her chest, "you're as quiet as a cat!" Instantly, she regretted having reminded the girl that her precious pet was still missing.

Her daughter-in-law stepped up to the sink and reached for the dish towel. "I'm glad I found you alone," she said, grabbing a pot from the drainboard. "There's something I need to tell you. It's been keeping me up nights and—" Eyes wide, she gasped and leaned closer. "Mom, you're…you're *bleeding!* Oh, Mom…I'm *so* sorry! If I hadn't startled you…"

"It isn't your fault, sweetie. I'm the one who shoved her hand into the water without—"

"Like I don't have enough to be sorry for," she muttered to herself. "Now this!" She wrapped the towel around Nadine's gash. "I took a first aid class while I was pregnant with Amy," she said, chattering nervously as she led Nadine to the powder room. "So I'd know how to handle childhood emergencies. I learned how to make a butterfly—"

Lamont appeared from out of nowhere. "What in tarnation happened?"

"Just a little dishwashing accident," Nadine explained, waving him away. "I'm in good hands. Nurse Julie, here, is going to fix me right up."

He stepped between the women, grabbed Nadine's hand and peeked under the towel. "Nice clean cut," he said, studying the cut, "but it's long. And deep. Needs a butterfly bandage." Replacing the towel, he said to Julie, "There's a roll of sterile gauze and a bottle of peroxide upstairs, in the linen closet." And opening the medicine cabinet, he added, "Will you get it, in case there isn't enough in here?"

Nodding, the girl rushed off, looking like a child caught in the act of stealing cookies before supper. Was the expression related to whatever she'd started to tell Nadine before the mishap in the dishwater or a reaction to Lamont's abrupt dismissal? "Really, Lamont," she began, "Julie was all set to—"

But he was too focused on the task at hand to hear her. Holding her hand over the basin, he poured peroxide over the cut. "Sting?"

"Not much." Well, at least her mini-emergency had served the purpose of bridging the tense gap between them.

In moments, he'd dabbed antibiotic ointment onto the cut, wrapped it with gauze and taped it with white adhesive. "There," he said. "Almost good as new."

"Thanks." She inspected her bandage-fat hand. "Why do you suppose Julie never came back?"

Shrugging, he returned the materials to the cabinet. "Probably couldn't find the gauze. Or maybe

Amy needed something. I thought I heard her up there earlier, splashing in the bathtub."

And for the second time in as many minutes, Nadine wondered what, exactly, had been keeping Julie up nights.

Chapter Nine

Frank's office looked a lot like the man, himself—lean, with very few embellishments.

Along one wall, two low filing cabinets supported a sheet of aging plywood, where yellowing newspapers, tattered file folders and an assortment of pens stood in half a dozen coffee mugs. The other wall boasted an open-doored closet whose shelves sagged under the weight of bloated banker's boxes marked OPEN and CLOSED. A huge orange cat lounged on the spare seat, one green eye opened halfway to study the stranger in the doorway.

Back to the door and booted feet propped on the wide windowsill, a balding man rocked in an oversized black chair, tapping a pencil eraser to the file in his lap. "Have a seat," he said, twirling the writing tool like a baton.

Lamont stepped up to the battered wooden desk. "I would if I could find one."

Both boots hit the floor as the chair whirled away from the bank of windows. "Well, look what the cat dragged in," Frank said, standing. "And speaking of cats…Winston, where are your manners? Get up so this old man can take a load off." With a bored yawn and an exaggerated stretch, the tabby leaped from the chair and settled atop the cluttered plywood.

Frank topped off his coffee. "Care for a cup?"

Lamont sat, ankle upon knee, and hung his Stetson from the toe of his boot. "Thanks, but I've had my quota for the day."

The men spent the next five minutes catching up, and then Frank leaned back in his chair. "So, what brings you to downtown Amarillo."

A statement, Lamont noticed, not a question. "Couple things I need you to check out."

"Couple of things for you, or—"

"For a friend."

He didn't know what made him pause, or why the hesitation prompted the guarded expression on Frank's narrow face. But rather than waste time speculating, Lamont launched into the reasons for his visit. As he described the fire, Nadine's financial situation, her son's money troubles and his concerns roused by her ranch hand and so-called pal, Jim, the detective fired up his computer, nodding and scribbling on a blue-lined tablet. "Ever consider that maybe the daughter-in-law had something to do with the fire?"

The thought had crossed his mind, but he'd quickly dismissed it. "What makes you say that?"

"Well," he said, pointing at the monitor, "says here the dealership never found out what happened to that money...and that the only reason they didn't press charges was because of her relationship to Nadine Greene."

"Why would *that* make any difference?"

"Miz Greene's husband was the dealership owner's first cousin."

"I don't see the connection. What's that got to do with your notion that Julie started the fire?"

"If I was young and stupid enough to lose fifty grand, my job and every dime in my personal savings and checking accounts," Frank said, "I'd probably want to do something to ease my conscience." He held out both hands, palms up. "What better way than a big fat insurance claim?"

"You're not makin' a lick of sense, Frank. The house was Nadine's, and the policy is in her name, not her boy's. What would be the point of Julie—"

"She was living with the mother-in-law before the house was torched, right?"

"Yeah, so?"

"So, maybe she saw this as a way to guarantee

that the little widow was set for life, and in the process, guaranteed the same thing for herself, and the son and grandkid, too."

"I think you've watched too many movies," Lamont said. But he was only half joking. He thought back on broken dishes and knickknacks, furniture dings and scratches in his hardwood—all caused by Julie's ham-fisted actions. "She's scatterbrained enough to have started a fire, I'll grant you that, but I doubt she could figure out how to do it on purpose. Not without burning herself to a crisp in the process, anyway. Besides, the poor kid spent half her life in foster homes, and thinks of Nadine more as a mother than a mother-in-*law*. She knows as well as any of us that if the fire marshal decides to prosecute, Nadine could go to jail." He watched Frank print LONDON in big black letters on the tab of a manila folder. "So even if she *did* start out with a mind to getting what she saw as 'easy money,' I can't see her letting Nadine take the rap for it."

Frank tore his notes from his tablet and slid the pages into the file. "Go with your gut," he said. "I learned the hard way it'll rarely steer you wrong."

He referred, Lamont knew, to that awful night in New York City, when second-guessing had cost Frank his partner, ended his career in law enforcement and left him with a bum leg. Unsnapping the pearl button on the pocket of his Western shirt, Lamont withdrew a slip of paper that had been folded in half, and in half again. On it, he'd written everything he knew about Jim the ranch hand. "Isn't much, but maybe it'll give you a starting point."

Nodding, Frank read the name and address, and added it to Lamont's file. "When do you want me to dig in?"

"Yesterday?"

"You're in luck. I just closed a case day before." He punched a few more keys on his computer, and the screen lit up with a twelve-by-seven-inch color photo of Winston, sunning himself on the red-flowered cushions of a wicker chair. "Let me pull up my accounting program, and we'll talk dollars per hour."

"What—you're not gonna do this as a favor for an old friend?"

"Is the '65 Cor—"

Lamont groaned. "Just name your price and spare me the Corvette talk."

"She's right outside," Frank said, tapping a photo of the car. "You're dying to see her. I know you are."

Lamont got to his feet. "Tell you what. You

drive, and I'll buy lunch so we can, ah, hammer out the particulars."

Frank's eyes lit up with mischief as he grabbed his keys. "Deal," he said, limping toward the door.

"I hate to impose," Lamont's daughter, Cammi, said into the phone, "but Reid and I haven't been out alone since before Rosie was born."

Nadine had no idea where Cammi's father had gone, or how long he'd be away. After three unanswered calls to his cell phone, she said, "I'm sure your dad will be thrilled to spend some time with his little granddaughter. Besides," she added, "it'll be fun for Amy, and for Julie, too." It was certainly true. The wide-eyed innocence of children had a tendency to make life's troubles pale by comparison.

"You're the greatest, the absolute greatest. I don't know why Dad doesn't just carry you off to the pastor's office and set a date."

Now how was she supposed to respond to *that?* Thankfully, Cammi launched into the list of baby things they'd bring along, leaving Nadine to wonder who else might feel the same way. His other daughters? Neighbors? Surely not Lamont!

She decided to distract herself from the subject by getting Cammi's old room ready for Rosie's visit. It had been a long time since she'd fawned over a baby. Almost five years, to be exact. If Adam and Julie didn't soon get a handle on their marital problems, Amy might be her only shot at grandparenting, so she intended to make the most of every minute.

When dusting and vacuuming didn't put the question to rest, she focused her concentration on chopping potatoes, carrots, beans and beef for the stew pot. She was half in, half out of the fridge, clearing a shelf for formula and jars of baby food, when the whistled notes of "Texas, Our Texas" warned her of Lamont's approach.

"Something smells mighty good in here," he said, sniffing his way into the room. "I just had a huge breakfast in town, so I hope that isn't lunch."

"Oh? In town with whom?"

Lamont grabbed an apple from the basket on the counter and bit into it. "Macintosh," he said as he chewed. "My favorite."

Had he made a conscious decision not to tell her where or with whom he'd been? Or had his blasé manner simply made it seem that way? Caring for him and his house might well be wifely work, but since he hadn't yet dragged her to the pastor's office, as Cammi had suggested, what business was it of hers?

The word *yet* ricocheted from her head to her

heart and back again, making her more aware than ever that if she didn't put some serious effort into tamping down her feelings for him, she was in for a world of hurt. "Cammi and Reid are dropping the baby off in a few minutes. Isn't that great? She gets to spend the whole night with her grand-dad!"

He gave her a look that made her blood ran cold.

"You're joking."

Nadine added dry mustard to the stew, and gave it a good stir. "One of Reid's buddies is getting married," she explained, "and he asked Reid to be an usher. Cammi says they never expected this guy—Tommy, I think that was his name—to settle down, so—"

Lamont stepped up beside her, one hand on the counter, palmed his apple in the other. His grim expression and stiff-backed stance made it clear that he hoped she was, indeed, joking, either about Tommy finally making a commitment or Rosie's overnight visit.

"The kids haven't been out alone in months," she continued. "I used my cell phone to call yours while she and I were talking, but after three tries, I gave up. I didn't know if you'd turned yours off or if you were out of range." She sounded so much like a nagging housewife, even to herself, that she snapped her mouth shut. "You *did* get my message, didn't you?"

The taut line of his lips relaxed—but only slightly—as he processed the information. "Never gave a thought to check voice mail, since the phone never rang." Frowning, he unpocketed it and snapped it open. "Well, I'll be," he said, "there it is, plain as day."

She'd heard that tone before, it was the one that warned her when Ernest was about to give her the third degree. "I couldn't imagine you'd turn Cammi down," she said defensively, "so I agreed to keep the baby. Besides, remember how just the other day you were saying how much you miss spending time with her?"

What was going on in that head of his? And why was he standing there, glaring as if she'd just backed his pickup into the side of the house? *"Mi casa, su casa,"* he'd said on the day she moved in. Until now, it seemed he'd meant it. But what if, instead, it had been one of those "Do as you please…once it meets with my approval" offers? "Rosie won't be a bother," she said. "I'll take care of everything."

"I adore that li'l gal, and you're right, it kills me that I don't get to see a whole lot more of her." He tossed the apple core into the trash can and began to pace, slant-heeled boots thudding across the hardwood. He stopped not two feet from where she stood. "It's just that I'm concerned for her safety."

"For Rosie's safety?" she repeated. "You're worried that I'd let something happen to her?"

He slapped a hand to the back of his neck and thundered, "Of course not." Then, softening his tone a mite, Lamont attempted a smile—though it never quite reached those glittering gray orbs. "For cryin' out loud, Nadine, quit looking so terrified. I'd *never* hurt you, not for any reason or in any way. If you don't know that by now, we're both in a heap o' trouble."

She believed him—or wanted to, anyway. "Sorry," she admitted. "I never should have said yes to such a thing without talking to you first. Cammi's your daughter and this is your house. I had no right to—"

"You think I was lying?"

"About what?"

"When I said this is your home, too, for as long as you need it to be."

She shook her head and, summoning a sliver of courage, met his eyes. "I don't get it."

"There's nothing to *get*. Maybe I'm an idiot, thinking there's a chance that what happened at your house could happen here, while my li'l granddaughter is upstairs, asleep."

So Lamont didn't mind risking his own skin to save her life, to make a home for her and her kids, but he drew the line at putting anyone else in jeopardy. And who could blame him. "Oh, Lamont," she said, "I'm sorry, so sorry! I'm the one who's an idiot!" If she ever figured out what she'd done in her trifling life to deserve a friend like him, Nadine would do it over and again, to ensure he'd always be part of her life. Unadulterated affection merged with gratitude. If only she could show him how much she appreciated everything he'd done, and everything he was.

The back door opened with a *whoosh,* and Cammi and Reid breezed into the kitchen. As Rosie reached for her grandfather, Nadine started a pot of coffee.

She didn't share Marcus's opinion that the fire at her house had been set on purpose, but what if she was wrong?

Nadine intended to stay awake until Lamont's daughter and her family were snug in their own home, just in case.

Chapter Ten

Alone in Cammi's old bedroom, Nadine continued rocking Rosie, even though she'd finished her
bottle and burped half an hour ago. Facing the big
window seat, shards of the moon's brilliant white
light slanted though the French doors, where gauzy
curtains fluttered in the early June breeze.

Holding a baby in her arms again felt good,
so good that it inspired a contented sigh. Nadine
leaned against the chair's pillowy backrest and
studied the long eyelashes that dusted Rosie's
pink cheeks. She'd have freckles before she was
Amy's age, Nadine thought, picturing Cammi at
that age—a tinier, chubbier version of the beautiful young woman she'd become.

"I don't know why Dad doesn't just carry you
off and make you marry him," Cammi had said.
At the time, Nadine hadn't given it much thought,
but now, under the tranquil influence of soft baby

breaths and the mellow gleam of the strawberry moon, she smiled. Since the fire, she'd pretty much run his house single-handedly. How much different could it be as his wife?

With the child safely settled in her portacrib, Nadine picked up the baby monitor's receiver and tiptoed into the hall, leaving the door slightly ajar. Lamont always turned in by ten, and after a full day of caring for her dogs and goats and everything related to River Valley Ranch, she wasn't usually long behind him.

Tonight, though, Nadine didn't feel the least bit sleepy and decided to get into her pajamas and join Adam and Julie in the family room. On the way, she looked in on her granddaughter. Always a fitful sleeper, Amy had kicked off her covers and dropped her favorite teddy bear on the floor. Smiling, Nadine tucked the sheets under the girl's chin and lay the stuffed bear beside her. "Now I lay you down to sleep," Nadine whispered, bending to kiss the girl's forehead, "and pray the Lord your soul to keep, while His angels watch you through the night, and keep you in their blessed sight, Amen." After a last glance, Nadine slipped from the room.

As she made her way down the hall, Nadine noticed that Adam and Julie's door was shut tight, and not even a glimmer of light shone from beneath it. They'd said at dinner that they might turn in early and, evidently, they'd done just that. A tiny thrill went through her, because she couldn't remember the last time she had an hour all to herself. She'd brew herself a cup of herbal tea, then find an upbeat old movie on cable.

Ten minutes later, Nadine padded into the family room on white-socked feet, a steaming mug of tea in one hand, the baby monitor's receiver in the other, all ready to settle in for a little peace and quiet. The sight of Lamont, slouched in his buttery leather recliner, stopped her in her tracks and she nearly slopped hot tea onto her hand.

"I thought you'd gone to bed an hour ago."

"Couldn't sleep." He gave a nod toward her cup. "Whatcha got there?"

"Mandarin orange tea." She held out the mug. "Here, you take this one. The water's still hot. I'll fix myself another cup."

While waiting for the kettle to whistle, she sliced cheese and apples onto a plate and pictured him, slumped in front of the TV in his maroon "Fightin' Aggie" sweatpants and matching T-shirt. And if her eyes hadn't been playing tricks on her, the slippers bore his alma mater's logo, too. Funny, but he looked every bit as dashing as he had in his tux at Lily's wedding.

"What's this?" he said, sitting up when she carried the plate into the room.

"I noticed that you didn't eat much at supper tonight, so I thought you might like a little something to tide you over until breakfast." She handed him the platter, then stood the baby monitor's receiver atop a stack of coloring books. "How's your tea?" she asked, curling up on the end of the sofa. "Sweet enough?"

He took a sip and said, "Perfect." Then he got to his feet, and in one giant step, climbed over the coffee table. "Nothin' worse than snacking alone." After constructing a tower of cheese and crackers, he grinned. "Du-wu-shush," he said around the mouthful. "Shum-pree du-wu-shush."

Laughing, Nadine said, "Didn't your mother teach you that it isn't polite to talk with your mouth full?"

Licking his lips, he began assembling another stack. "Yeah," he said with a wink, "as a matter of fact, she did." He punctuated the admission with a merry wink.

"Oh, but I'll bet you were a handful as a boy!"

"Let's just say she got plenty of exercise, chasing me with that old wooden spoon of hers."

He'd never talked about his childhood before. Which was curious, since he knew so much about her life. And her son's. Nadine pressed for more information. "Did she ever use it? The spoon, I mean."

"Just once." He took a sip of tea. "She'd invited a bunch of her friends over—somebody's baby shower, as I recall—and covered every flat space in the kitchen with cookies and pies and cakes."

"And you ate something without permission?"

"Couple of somethings, actually, but that isn't what earned me a whippin'." He leaned back on the cushion beside her. "See, I'd clean forgot about her party, and after baseball practice, I invited the team over for a snack." Leaning forward, he assembled another stack. "I tell you, the boys, they laid into just about every pastry they could get their grimy hands on. So by the time Mama and her gal pals came in to serve up those tasty treats…" He chuckled as he popped an apple slice into his mouth. "Let's just say she wasn't very happy…"

"Good grief," Nadine said, laughing. "I can almost picture that, from the boys' perspective, and your poor mother's, too."

He began creating a third tower. "Sounded like a henhouse in there, and those kids ran off so fast, they left heelprints on the seat of their pants!"

"Guess you had a hard time sitting on *yours* once all the ladies went home."

Eyes wide, Lamont nodded. "Talk about your understatements!"

He held the last cheese-and-crackers stack between thumb and forefinger, turning it right, then left. It wasn't until he narrowed his eyes and smirked that she understood what he aimed to do with it. "Don't even think about it, mister."

One hand resting on the sofa's back, the other elbow pressing into the back cushion, Lamont effectively trapped Nadine. "I noticed that *you* didn't eat much at supper tonight, either." He waved the food under her nose.

By the tender age of eight, Nadine had learned that the best way to discourage worm-toting boys on the playground was to pretend she *liked* worms and bugs. They quickly grew bored with the girl who wasn't afraid of slimy things, and found other girls to torment. If the idea worked then, why wouldn't it work now?

She opened her mouth wide to accept the treat, and the instant his handiwork disappeared, he returned to his spot on the couch. "Aw," he said, chuckling as she munched away, "you're no fun at all."

"Sorry."

He turned slightly and, for the longest time, just sat there, gawking at her. Finally she said, "What?"

A slow, easy grin spread across his face. "Can't

a guy just take a minute to thank God for all that's good in his life?"

Nadine had no time to formulate an answer, for he pulled her to him and tenderly held her face in his hands. She'd seen many expressions on his handsome face, but this? She hadn't seen this one before. What inspired the glint in those gray orbs, the lift of his brows, the odd angle of his grin? Most striking of all, she noticed a slight tremor in his usually steady hands.

One question stood out among the rest: Did he truly believe she'd started that fire? It was bad enough, knowing that Marcus and others down at City Hall thought she'd burned down her own house, but the idea that *Lamont* might agree? Well, it saddened her to the point of tears.

Pressing both palms against his chest, Nadine tried to break free of his embrace. "I need to—"

"Shh," he said, laying a callused finger over her lips.

His words and actions sometimes brought back disturbing memories of her years with Ernest, but oddly enough, Lamont made her feel safe and cared for, too. Made her feel more like a woman than she'd ever felt. Surely those were good signs, signs that he could be trusted with her heart.

His arms encircled her and she closed her eyes, trying not to think about the fact that she carried more emotional baggage than the suitcase handlers at the airport. Did he realize what a colossal mistake it would be, linking himself to her?

Cammi's words echoed in her head yet again, "Why doesn't Dad just marry you?"

Letting herself fall for him had been crazy. Hoping he felt the same way, well, that was crazier still. But the craziest thought of all? That if Lamont *were* to pop the question, she'd say yes, even though she felt one hundred percent certain of how unfair it would be to saddle him with her problems and predicaments.

If she truly cared for him, wouldn't she send him packing—for his own good?

"What's going on in that pretty head of yours?"

Nadine didn't trust herself to talk.

The clock gonged the half hour. "There's a movie about the life of C. S. Lewis starting right now."

"But it's eleven-thirty, and you have to get up early tomorrow."

"So do you. Besides, I never promised to stay awake while you watch it."

Grinning despite her dark thoughts, Nadine reached for her mug. "You're out of your mind, you know."

"Yeah," he said, snuggling up beside her, "I know."

Lamont didn't fall asleep, and neither did Nadine. While the movie flickered silently on the

TV screen, they talked. Then moved to the kitchen to make sandwiches and more tea, and talked some more. They might have talked until the sun came up if a nightmare hadn't roused Amy, who shuffled sleepy-eyed into the room and climbed into Nadine's lap.

Chapter Eleven

He didn't like looking at the empty chair where she'd sat, so Lamont sneaked upstairs to see what was taking so long.

Even before reaching the baby's bedroom door, he heard her, softly humming a tune he recognized but couldn't quite place. Lamont froze in his tracks, not wanting to risk that his heavy footfalls would set off that annoying creak in the floor. When his own girls were small, he'd promised Rose that he'd fix it, and by the time they reached their teens, he thanked the good Lord that he hadn't, because it never failed to signal him when they stayed out past their curfew.

"I believe in miracles," she sang. "I've seen a soul set free, miraculous the change in one redeemed through Calvary…I've seen the lily push its way through stubborn sod, I believe in miracles, for I believe in God…"

When he was a boy, his mother had sung it to him, and whether thunderstorms or scary dreams or monsters under his bed were the cause of his fears, the song never failed to calm him. He held his breath, hoping Nadine would sing the next verse, and the next. But he only heard the quiet creak of the rocking chair.

He'd intended to catch a peek, then go back downstairs. But when he poked his head around the doorframe and saw her sitting there, silhouetted by the amber radiance of the nightlight, Lamont felt as if somebody had nailed his boots to the floor.

Eyes closed, she cradled his precious, peacefully sleeping grandchild in her arms. For many lonesome years, Lamont had loved Nadine from afar, but never more than at this moment. He knew that for certain now, though it wasn't likely he'd live long enough to puzzle out why it had taken him so long to acknowledge it—but never more than at this moment.

"What's going on in that handsome head of yours, cowboy?"

He walked softly into the room and crouched beside the chair. He must have reached too quickly to tuck a curl behind Rosie's ear, because Nadine shrank back, eyes shut tight and one hand up, as if to defend herself from a slap, or worse.

Instinct made him want to pummel the man who, even after years in the grave, could still inspire such a reaction in her. "Nadine, darlin'," he said, voice raspy from holding back the sob her fear had induced, "remember when I said I'd never hurt you?"

Instantly, Nadine assumed her "Everything is fine" expression. "Don't mind me," she whispered, grinning. "Sometimes I'm as jumpy as a grasshopper. I should probably quit drinking caffeinated coffee."

"Don't give me that. You can't pretend forever that he didn't... That none of it happened."

"None of *what?*"

"The beatings." There—he'd said it. Now let her try to deny that Ernest hadn't abused her.

"I never wanted anyone to—"

"...let not the foot of pride come against me..."

She blew a puff of air through her lips. "Wasn't *pride* that made me want to keep it a secret," she said dully, "it was *shame*."

He had to look away, long enough, at least, to ask for the wisdom to know which words would comfort and reassure her. "Shame? But why?"

"Because I chose poorly."

Despite his prayer, her words didn't make sense.

"I ran off with the first good-looking boy who paid any attention to me. I never asked the good

Lord what *He* intended for me." Her lovely mouth formed a thin, taut smile. "I figured those years were penance of a sort. Until I grew up, and realized that isn't how God works."

"Glad to hear you came to your senses, but where did you get a cockeyed notion like that in the first place, you gorgeous, brave, amazing, bighearted, nutty woman, you?"

"Why, Lamont London," she whispered, "are you trying to sweep me off my feet with poetic praise?"

"Harrumph. I forgot to add *funny* to the list."

"To answer your question, I got the cockeyed notion from my mother. She popped in for an unexpected visit once, about an hour after, a…you know…and when she saw the cuts and bruises, she reminded me that chastisements are a form of love. And discipline, she said, can't be achieved without first instilling fear."

"Your mom sounds like a real gem."

"Oh, don't be too hard on her. She lived a tough life. And if you want my honest opinion, I think that was her way of rationalizing why she tolerated the same thing from my dad."

"Makes me sick, just sick, to know that bigger, stronger people are willing to use people as punching bags, all in the name of love."

She tucked in one corner of her mouth and lifted

a shoulder. "Well, the main thing is, we survived. And stopped the cycle."

"Ah, darlin'," he said, brushing a bent forefinger across her cheek, "if I could erase it all, I would."

She looked at him for a long time, making Lamont wish he had the power to read minds, at least for those few moments. Because he would have given anything to assure himself that glitter in her eyes and the downturn of her mouth didn't mean she thought *he* was capable of such brutality.

And then she sighed. "You know, I think I believe you."

He made note of the fact that she'd tacked a qualifier onto the statement. It told him that while she didn't quite believe him now, she might someday. At least, he hoped she would.

She met his eyes to say, "You're a good and decent man, Lamont. Have I told you how much I appreciate everything you've done for us?"

"Only about ten thousand times."

Smiling, she said, "But have I told you lately?"

Eyes narrowed, he scratched his chin. "I believe you said something along those lines yesterday at breakfast. In plain English." He pressed a palm to her cheek. "But you say it every minute of every day, in a thousand different ways, when you're tossing my favorite foods into the grocery cart and folding my bandanas just so, and—"

"I have to get out of here—the sooner, the better."

Now, why'd she have to go and spoil the moment with a crack like that? "No. You don't."

"Yes, I do, because I'm…" She bit her lower lip.

Falling in love with me? he hoped. He knew that look. If he didn't come up with some logical, practical reason for her to stay—and do it quick—she might just make good on her threat. "You gave your word that with Peggy gone, you'd help me out around here. Besides, if you leave, your kids will, too. And where would they go?"

He watched her brows inch closer together as she processed that thought. Lamont scooted closer. "Give it time, Nadine, okay? And patience. Before you know it, you'll have the insurance check and you can interview contractors and talk to an architect and—"

"Can't do any of that from a jail cell."

It broke his heart to hear the wooden tone in her voice. "That'll never happen."

"Oh? You have some pull down at City Hall, do you?" And then she kissed Rosie's forehead.

He considered all the things he might say, and since not one of them would ease her mind,

Lamont decided to pick up the conversation later. Maybe Frank would come up with something that would clear Nadine's name.

The baby stirred slightly, and because he'd positioned himself so near, one chubby hand plopped against his cheek. "Will you please put that baby to bed, before our jabbering wakes her?"

Surprisingly, she did as he'd asked.

In the hall, Nadine said, "You know what?"

"What?"

"I believe you."

And then she hurried toward her room and left him standing outside Rosie's door, alone and lonely and confused, trying to remember what he'd said to inspire her parting comment.

Adam sat on the couch, a single sheet of notepaper dangling from his trembling fingertips. "I don't get it," he said, driving a hand through his hair. "Has she lost her ever-lovin' *mind?*"

Lamont sat on the coffee table facing the boy. "Mind if I have a look?" he asked as Nadine sat beside him.

Dear God, she prayed, *let it be a mistake. A silly, misunderstanding...*

"Dear Adam," Lamont began, "I can't live this way anymore, knowing how much you despise and mistrust me. You're a wonderful father, so there isn't a doubt in my mind that you'll take good care of Amy. And just think, without me in the picture, you'll never have to worry that she'll pick up any of my bad habits and grow up to disappoint you, the way I have.

"Please tell your mom how much I appreciate all she's done for me over the years, and tell her that I'm sorry for everything she's going through because of me. Thank Lamont, too, for welcoming me into his home. I don't deserve the kindness and patience you've all shown, but I'm grateful for it, just the same. Believe it or not, I'm doing this because I love you all so very much."

Now it was Lamont who ran a hand through his hair. "It isn't signed," he said, handing the note to Nadine.

She nearly wept, herself, when she saw the childlike script, and the tears Julie had drawn on the smiley-faced heart at the bottom of the page. There had been dozens of times when she'd noticed the girl, huddled on the sofa, looking alone and afraid, though the rest of them were in the room with her. She'd ignored every maternal instinct that told her that a hug or a kind word might comfort Julie, because she didn't want Adam thinking she'd taken sides. Why hadn't she done the right thing, even if it meant upsetting her son? He'd always been a resilient boy and would have recovered quickly. "Did she pack a suitcase?"

"Don't know" was Adam's glum reply. "Found the note sitting on top of Amy's coloring book, like a little white tent with stupid, ugly news inside it."

He was hurting and confused, but there'd be plenty of time to comfort him later on. Right now, it was far more important to find Amy and try to talk some sense into her. "I'll check," Nadine said.

She raced up the steps, praying the whole way that when she reached the kids' room, Julie would be sprawled out on the bed, reading or sleeping or even crying into her pillow was better than *not* finding her!

But the bedcovers were tidy and smooth, and Julie's favorite red backpack wasn't on the hook behind the door, where she'd kept it since they'd moved into Lamont's house. Almost-full dresser drawers meant she'd taken only what would fit into the bag. Not much. Certainly not enough to last more than a few days.

"Good news," she said upon entering the family room, "she probably hasn't gone far, and I doubt she'll be gone long, either."

Adam met her eyes. "What makes you say that?"

"She only packed a few things." She sat beside

him, gave his shoulder a comforting squeeze. "What do you bet she'll be home before dark?"

Her son nodded. "Is Amy in her room?"

"Coloring," Nadine said, "and listening to her nursery rhymes CD."

Another nod. "Good. That'll give me time to think."

"About...?"

"About what to tell her when she asks why her *mother* won't be here to tuck her in tonight."

Frank arrived at the coffee shop ten minutes late. Red-faced and panting, he slid into the booth seat across from Lamont's and slapped a thick file folder onto the table. "One of these days, somebody's gonna figure out how to eliminate traffic jams."

"The guy who does that," Lamont said, "will get rich quick."

Frank waved the waitress over. "Roads are under the control of local government. When have you ever known anything to happen 'quick' when bureaucrats are involved?" He ordered eggs and bacon, hash browns, tomato juice and coffee. "What's *your* pleasure," he asked, "since it's your tab?"

Laughing, Lamont asked for a refill on his

coffee. "Nadine whipped up a rib-stickin' breakfast. Couldn't eat another bite if I tried."

"Harrumph," Frank said, smirking.

"What?"

"You never struck me as the 'playing house' type, is all."

Playing house? As if his mood wasn't already foul enough after finding out this morning that she'd given her bug-loving buddy Jim permission to hole up in her barn all this time, and the Julie-gone-missing episode adding to the mess. "As I told you, it's a temporary arrangement. Couldn't be avoided, 'cause after the fire, she had no place else to go. And neither did her kids."

"Mmm-hmm," he said around a mouthful of coffee.

"She's upstairs, clear at one end of the house, I'm downstairs at the other end."

"Methinks thou doth protest too much."

Lamont frowned. Frank had a point. A good one. Why *had* he felt so compelled to defend himself?

"So you really don't care what folks are saying?"

Did that mean Frank had heard things? Lamont harrumphed. "I've never been one to put much stock in what people think. There's only one opinion that matters to me." Using his thumb, he pointed

Heavenward. Though, in truth, what Nadine thought and felt mattered almost as much.

The waitress approached, and Frank slid his cup and the file aside to make room for the piled-high plate she carried. He waited until she moved to the next table, then tapped the file folder. "Dug up some pretty interesting stuff." Peeling a butter tab, he added, "And along the way, got some insights into this li'l gal's mother-in-law."

Insights? Double-talk wasn't Frank's style. Which either meant he hadn't found anything worth discussing, or he was trying to avoid telling Lamont some awful truth.

Frank bit the point from a slice of toast. "People talk," he said around it, "and sometimes what they say ain't all that flattering."

Now he wished he'd asked for a refill on his coffee, because sipping it would give him something to do besides gawk at the detective. "Anything negative you heard about Nadine is bunk. I'd bet the ranch on it."

"Okay, so you're nuts about her. Point made and taken." He shrugged. "But in my business, you see a lot of proof that when love talks, it doesn't always tell the truth. So all right, fall in love, get married, refill that mansion of yours with more babies, even, if that flips your Stetson." He rested an elbow on the table, used his fork as a pointer.

"Just don't be one of those guys who's stupid in love. You didn't work a lifetime to throw it all away for a pretty face."

Frank picked up a strip of bacon and was about to snap off a bite when Lamont said, "You still a prayin' man, Frank?"

"Bum knee, remember?"

"It's been *my* experience that a man can pray standing, sitting or flat on his face."

He speared a potato and popped it into his mouth. "We go too far back to spar over religion, m'friend. How I pray, *if* I pray, is my business, and let's just leave it at that."

Lamont nodded. "Fair enough. But by the same token, how I live my life—and who I share it with—is *my* business."

Frank downed his glass of tomato juice, blotted his lips on a paper napkin then shoved the file to Lamont's side of the table. "I don't think you're gonna like paying me for the dirt I dug up."

"On Nadine?"

Shaking his head, Frank said, "On that daughter-in-law of hers. Seems she's gone missing before. Couple of times, matter of fact."

"Where'd you get this information?"

"It's better for you if you don't know the details. Let's just say I have friends in high places, friends who helped me turn over a rock or two, and helped me unlock a few top-secret file drawers." He leaned back, stretched both arms across the back of his seat. "Remember when I asked you if you thought sweet little Julie might have had anything to do with your girlfriend's house burning down?"

Lamont nodded, and let the "girlfriend" reference slide.

"Well, if she *isn't* responsible, I'll eat my hat."

Not good news, for anybody involved. "You're not wearing a hat."

"So I'll buy one." He winked. "And add it to your bill."

Lamont had only locked his office door on one other occasion—the night Rose died. He'd come home from the hospital feeling lost and spent and heartbroken and, after making sure his motherless girls were sound asleep in their rooms, sequestered himself behind the soundproof walls, because the last thing they needed was to hear his anguished sobs.

This time, he'd entered the room feeling angry, agitated and confused. He snapped the blinds shut and flipped the bolt, then flicked on his desk lamp and sat down to study Julie's file.

For starters, her name *wasn't* Julie Greene.

Born Carla Cassidy in Detroit, she'd entered

the Michigan foster care system when her parents were killed in a head-on crash. By the time the girl turned twelve, she'd lived with seven families. At thirteen, her counselors finally found a good match, and Carla settled in with a mom and dad who, in addition to three other kids, raised carrier pigeons. She loved tending the birds, Carla told one therapist, especially the hatchlings. Enjoyed it so much, in fact, that she didn't even mind the odious chore of cleaning the coop floors.

The girl's happy life ended abruptly when illness put her in the hospital. Diagnosed with cryptococcal meningitis, she spiked a fever of 106.5, and it took days for doctors to get the infection under control. Upon returning home, Carla could no longer perform routine tasks. Over the next months, she withdrew from friends and family. One day might find her huddled in a corner, barely able to utter two words. And the next, verbal outbursts and physical attacks on her siblings were her norm.

Pushed to the limits of their parenting skills, her foster parents sought out a child specialist who blamed the high fever for Carla's paranoid schizophrenia. Thorazine was prescribed, but when her behavior turned violent, institutionalization was required. Through the haze of medication, she overheard the escape plans of fellow patients and, determined to join them, Carla hid her meds in the heating vent. Then late one night, she slid aside a manhole cover on the hospital grounds and followed the storm drain to the city streets.

Her photo made the evening news, inspiring 911 reports of a young girl stealing clothes from a sidewalk sale. Before long, she found herself on the wrong side of wire-and-glass windows, telling her story to a white-coated therapist who administered tried-and-true therapies, and a few that were brand new. The scenario repeated itself in Chicago and Buffalo, New York and Baltimore, yet no matter which drug or confinement methods the so-called experts tried, the innovative young woman managed to escape.

Lamont closed the file, remembering what Frank had said in the diner that morning. "She must've gone into remission. Happens sometimes with schizophrenics. I expect that's why Nadine's boy didn't realize anything was wrong with her when they met. Can't imagine any other reason the kid would've married a nutjob like that."

At the time, Frank's choice of words had made him cringe. Now—though still uncomfortable with the term nutjob—he had to admit that the detective's theory made about as much sense as anything else.

Something nagged at him, though—something

worrisome and terrifying. While most schizophrenics prefer being alone and rarely act out in aggressive or violent ways, the psychiatrist's last entry made it clear that Julie's particular brand of paranoia could manifest itself in suicidal or homicidal behaviors.

Shaking his head, Lamont tucked the file between two volumes of the encyclopedia and prayed that no one would find it there, because he needed time and Heavenly guidance to figure out when to share the information with Adam and Nadine.

Lamont pitied Julie—no question about it. And he'd do everything he could to help her…if only he could. But as the psychiatrist had written at least three times in Julie's file, "…there is no known cure for paranoid schizophrenia."

He didn't know whether or not Julie—or Carla or *whatever* her name was—had slipped from remission. Didn't know what she might be capable of, either. But he did know this: If she aimed to hurt Nadine or her son and granddaughter, he'd do whatever it took to stop her.

"Marcy Miller, with KAMR-TV 4," the familiar voice on the phone said, "calling to speak with Mr. London about Julie Greene."

When Julie didn't come home the night he'd found the note, Adam called the police. Following a cursory investigation, they apologized for the lack of information and leads, and said that they'd exhausted their resources. Desperate to find his troubled young wife, he decided to get the media involved, hoping an alert TV viewer would call in a "Julie sighting." So why had the pretty reporter asked for Lamont, and not Adam?

"I'm Julie's mother-in-law. Do you have information about her?"

"Couple of hours ago," she said, "I got a call from this guy, said he was a salesman in Abilene on business when he saw Julie's picture on the noon news. Said that, later, he saw her sitting on a bus stop bench. At least, he's thinks it was the same girl."

Abilene? If the salesman had seen Julie, how had she ended up more than 250 miles from home? Thoughts of everything that could happen to a confused young hitchhiker turned her blood to ice. "Did he say how she looked? Is she all right? Was she alone?"

"I know you're worried sick about her, and I'm sure your son and granddaughter are, too. That's why I called Sheriff Wallace, there in Amarillo, first thing. The minute I told him that Mr. London had hired a private detective he hit the roof because—in his words—'Those guys just muddy up the works!' So I suggested that maybe Mr. London had hired the man out of frustration with what the police were doing unfortunately, that didn't improve the sheriff's mood."

A private detective? Nadine couldn't think of a single reason why Lamont would keep such a thing from her. "Did you get the name of the man who saw Julie? Because if his information leads us to Julie, we'll want to thank him, of course."

"No…when he put me on hold to take another call, we were cut off. Just between you and me, the station manager is too cheap to spring for caller ID, so when the guy didn't call back, I had no way of finding him. I know the information seems sketchy, at best, and it might lead us nowhere but to a dead end. But sometimes, it takes us where we need to go. I hope that's the case here, because Julie looks like a sweet kid."

She *is* a sweet kid, Nadine thought, fighting tears. "I can't tell you how much we appreciate your involvement. I'll be sure to pass the message along to Mr. London when he gets home."

"You two married?" Marcy asked.

Nadine gave the reporter a quick rundown of the situation, being careful not to insert too many of the details as to why she and her kids had moved into Lamont's house.

"Sorry to hear all that, but I'm sure once the fire marshal completes his investigation, things will straighten out."

So much for keeping those facts under wraps. "How do you know I'm under investigation?"

"Police scanners," she said. "We don't miss much. Can't afford to."

Evidently not, Nadine thought. "Is there a number where Mr. London can reach you, in case his *detective* has any questions?"

Marcy rattled off the digits, then asked Nadine if she thought Adam might consent to an on-air interview. "Maybe Julie will see it, if she's still here, and make her way home on her own."

That hopeful notion made Nadine's heart soar. "I'm afraid that's a decision he'll have to make. I'll have him call you."

"And if Julie turns up?"

Not *when,* Nadine noted, heart sinking, but *if.*

As the call ended, Nadine wasn't sure which troubled her more—hearing that Julie had been spotted all the way down in Abilene or what Lamont's detective had uncovered. Her heart hammered, because only something dreadful could explain Lamont's secrecy.

Chapter Twelve

"I *wanted* to tell you," he admitted, "but I know you—too proud for your own good. You'd have seen it as a handout." He stopped pacing and shrugged. "You know what they say, it's easier to ask forgiveness than permission."

"It's not my forgiveness or permission you need. Julie is *Adam*'s wife. He's been a wreck since she disappeared, and Amy's a mess, too. Don't you think you should have talked it over with him, at least?"

"Talking with him is what gave me the idea in the first place."

She turned slightly at the top of the stepladder, dustrag in one hand, spray can of furniture polish in the other. "So let me get this straight—now you've got my *son* keeping secrets from me, too?"

Under normal circumstances, the question might not have sounded so angry and accusatory.

But these were far from normal circumstances. "Adam isn't keeping anything from you, because he doesn't know anything. I hired Frank on my own. To help him out. Because it drove me nuts to see how frustrated he was with the cops. Not that I blame him. I mean, those idiots have pretty much closed the case and don't have any qualms about admitting it."

Though he'd seen her dusting that same shelf not a week ago, she went at it again. Vigorously. "Every TV station in a five-state area—even the cable stations—are airing family photos." She spritzed the next shelf. "I can't believe this guy in Abilene is the only one who's seen her."

Lamont had no doubt that others had seen Julie. But just as he'd made the decision not to get involved in Nadine and Ernest's troubled marriage, those folks had opted to mind their own business, too.

One by one, Nadine replaced the books and framed photos she'd just dusted. "So tell me, when did you hire this *Frank* person?"

He couldn't very well tell her the truth. At least, not without admitting that what he'd *really* been looking for at the outset involved her weird friend Jim, not Julie. "A while ago."

"And why keep it from Adam?"

"Didn't know what Frank might find out, for one

thing." That much, at least, was true. "I didn't see any point in getting the boy's hopes up unless… *until* we had some credible information."

She moved a step higher on the ladder, and began cleaning the knickknacks on the top shelf.

"Nadine, come down from there, will you please? You could fall."

"I'm very sure-footed," she said. "Don't worry about me."

"Then how 'bout if you worry about *me?* You're making me a nervous wreck, watching you up there, acting like a trapeze artist."

"Tightrope walker, you mean," she said.

But at least she'd climbed down from her high perch.

She sat on the arm of the sofa, crossed her legs and rested the spray can on her knee. "So has your *Frank* come up with anything so far?"

Lamont put both hands in his pockets and rested his chin on his chest. Which was the right thing to do…tell Nadine about Julie's file now, or bring the girl's husband up to speed first? "How about if I spell it all out for you and Adam at the same time. This evening, maybe, after Amy's tucked in for the night."

Nadine's trembling voice betrayed her brave expression. "Is…is the news that bad?"

"I'll tell you this much, Julie has a very troubling background."

Now, in addition to dark circles under her eyes, worry lines drew a number eleven between her delicate brows.

"My heart just aches for Adam." Shoulders slumped, she added, "Guess he's in for a real eye-opener tonight, isn't he?"

"Don't worry about him, Nadine. That boy of yours is stronger than you think. Stronger, even, than *he* thinks he is." Smiling, Lamont said, "Let's not forget who his model at 'being brave and toughing things out' example has been his whole life."

"A month ago, if I'd gotten a compliment like that, I probably would have gone all bigheaded with pride, you know? But now?" She exhaled a long shaky breath. "All I can say is, if Adam inherited *my* backbone, he's in trouble. Big trouble. Because I've never felt more weak and spineless in my entire life."

"I can't name a soul who would've handled things as well as you have. You've got the constitution of a Clydesdale."

Raising one eyebrow, Nadine grinned a little. "I'm flattered. I think."

"Say, you haven't started supper yet, have you?" Maybe a night on the town would lift her spirits.

"There's a big pot of spaghetti sauce simmering on the back burner."

"I thought I smelled something fantastic when I came in."

"With your favorite…"

"Meatballs?"

She nodded.

"Reminds me of that church social, a couple years ago, when you brought your special recipe. I went back so many times for refills, I thought for sure Miz Higgins was gonna rap my knuckles with her wooden spoon."

She laughed softly. "And I remember something you probably don't even know. Mrs. Higgins said if she were ten years younger, she'd give you a run for your money."

Lamont laughed. "Then I guess I'm lucky she wasn't ten years younger, because I don't know if I would've had what it took to outrun her." Then, "I'll tell you something I *know* you don't know."

"What?"

"Rose had been gone a couple years by then, and I ended up spending half that night on my knees, begging God's forgiveness."

"Forgiveness?" She snickered. "Oh, now you're just making fun of me. There was plenty of spaghetti for everybody, even with your repeated visits to the buffet table."

"I'm not making fun of you, and that's the honest truth. I wasn't asking forgiveness for my gluttony."

"Then what?"

"I asked forgiveness because, all night long, every time I saw you clearing tables, filling plates, talking and laughing…the main thought that kept bouncing around in my head was…" Now that he'd gone this far, Lamont regretted opening this rusty old can. But, seeing no way to worm his way out of admitting the truth, he said, "I kept wishing you were *my* wife, not Ernest's."

"Just when I think there's no way you could embarrass me again, you say something like that."

"What, that you were responsible for my sinful thoughts?"

Gasping, Nadine clucked her tongue. "*You're* the one who should be embarrassed, saying such a thing!"

Lamont only grinned. "How much longer 'til supper's ready?"

She glanced at the mantel clock. "Couple of hours."

"I'll be in my office, if you need me for anything." He folded the stepladder and hoisted it onto one shoulder. "Take it easy for the rest of the day, will ya?"

He pretended not to have seen her "I'll do what

needs doing" expression and headed for the utility room. With the ladder back where it belonged, at least he wouldn't have to worry about her teetering on the highest step while he got cleaned up for supper.

Behind closed doors, he went to his bureau for a clean shirt, and caught himself staring at the family photos, all lined up in a tidy row on top of it. Rose in her wedding gown and him in a tux, Rose on their honeymoon on a beach in Cancun, Rose rocking Cammi in the chair that still sat in his oldest daughter's old room, Rose pregnant with the twins.

Across the room, on the dresser where she'd kept nightgowns and panty hose and the single strand of pearls he'd bought her on their first anniversary, more pictures. Rose with rollers in her hair, snapped on Christmas morning, and Rose sprawled on a blanket, feeding peanuts to a squirrel.

On the rolltop desk she'd found and refinished, Rose posing with half a dozen leading men she'd starred with, before giving up her glamorous Hollywood life to become a lowly rancher's wife.

The pictures had been here and there and everywhere for so long that he barely noticed them anymore. Especially since Nadine had become such an important part of his life.

Nadine…

It hit him like a sucker punch to the gut, and for the first time in recent memory, Lamont struggled with uncertainty. In his world, things were black or white, right or wrong. There were things that had to be done now, and things that could wait. But for the life of him, he couldn't make heads or tails of his feelings for Nadine. Not while he still felt such overpowering love for his sweet, beautiful Rose.

He picked up the last picture of her, taken at Violet and Ivy's sixth birthday party. He'd caught her by surprise, startling her as she tried to light the candles on the twins' cake, and she'd come at him with a fingerful of frosting, green eyes alight with mischief…and full-blown love. That memory brought him back to Lily's birth, when things went completely haywire in the delivery room, and he and the doctors—and especially Rose—thought she might not make it. "You'll need help with the girls," she'd said, clamping his hand in a grip so tight that his knuckles ached. "Not somebody who gets *paid* to cook and clean, either. They'll need a woman around, full time, to help them tie hair bows, and teach them how to talk and walk and sit like proper ladies."

When she rallied—God bless her spunky soul—he'd teased her about the morose speech, and she'd doubled up her little fist. "Don't you *dare* make fun of me, you big goof, you." And then she'd pretended to sock him on the jaw.

If only he'd known that that just a few short years later, they'd bicker about a dress he thought she'd paid way too much for, especially considering she had one just like it—with the sales tags still on it—in her closet. Furious because he'd pointed out, *again,* that if she kept it up, she'd land the lot of them in the poorhouse, she'd stormed out into the dark rainy night, shopping bag over one shoulder, designer purse over the other.

And run a red light.

Right into the path of a pickup truck that T-boned her car.

Killing her instantly.

He beat himself up for a long, long time, thinking that if he'd just let her keep the silly frock or, at the very least, if she'd waited until morning to return it, maybe she wouldn't have died. It took his eldest daughter to point out, years later, that Rose had a stubborn streak as wide as Texas itself. "If she had it in her head to go out," Cammi said, "you would have had to bind and gag her to keep her in."

The words were like healing balm, because they allowed him to let go of the guilt and the self-blame. But they didn't stop him from missing his Rose. "Missing you like crazy," he whispered, stroking the funny face in the photograph.

A quiet knock at his door brought him back to the present. "Hey," he said, opening it to Nadine.

She stood in the hall, a tidy stack of thick white towels in her arms. "Just thought I'd get these put away while I'm waiting to set the table."

It seemed as if she was afraid to come in, which made no sense to him, since she'd been doing it several times a week, to vacuum or dust or change his bed linens.

"I thought you were in your office."

"I was. Figured I'd catch a quick shower before we eat."

He stepped aside and, as she crossed to the master bathroom, Nadine glanced at the picture he held and looked away quickly. Her voice echoed in the big marble-and-glass space. "She was a striking woman, your Rose."

Lamont gawked at the photo, at the gaudy silver frame that held it. Suddenly, he felt like an idiot, standing there. Pivoting in a slow circle, he acknowledged that every week, as she tidied his room, Nadine had been forced to touch *and* see this shrine he'd built to his dead wife.

When she walked out of the bathroom, she was smiling, and it made his heart skip a beat. He should be used to that by now, as often as it happened. But he wasn't. Then he remembered his stubborn habit of deciding on some things right away. He'd been looking for a signal. Praying for a sign. The way she stood, backlit by the big overhead light, she reminded him—not for the first time—of an angel. If that wasn't it, then he didn't know *what* to look for!

"I'd better get the water boiling for the pasta," she announced, marching toward the hall.

As he closed the door behind her, one thought gonged in his head: Why wait? And Lamont read the question as the Lord's answer to his prayer.

Tonight, once the nasty business of Julie's file was behind them, he'd get on his knees. Again. This time to propose. If her answer was yes— and he hoped with everything in him that it would be—he'd slip a very special ring onto the third finger of her left hand.

In his top drawer, he found the wide gold band that had belonged to his paternal grandmother. A simple woman of deep faith, she'd given it to him, months before joining Rose in Paradise. "You'll fall in love again," she'd said, pressing it into his palm, "and when you do, I want you to give this to your bride."

He removed it from its minuscule black velvet pouch to look at the three small diamonds that symbolized faith, hope and love, and the fanciful inscription inside that quoted Ecclesiastes: "Two are better than one." And if Nadine would do him the honor of becoming his wife, he'd wear the matching band that his grandpa had designed for his grandmother.

"It's all in Your hands now, Lord," he whispered, pocketing the ring. "If she says no, bless me with the strength to hold it all together."

Because as God was his witness, Lamont didn't know how he'd get through the rest of his days without her.

Adam sat in stunned silence, shaking his head and running both hands through his hair. "I can't believe it," he said finally. "How could I have been so *wrong* about her?"

Nadine crossed the room and sat beside him, slid an arm across his shoulders. "You weren't wrong, honey. When you two met, Julie was—"

"Julie or Carla or Kristie—only God knows how many other aliases she's racked up over the years—seemed normal enough. I have to admit, there were signs. Plenty of them. But I wanted to be her hero so, like a fool, I ignored them."

"Whatever she did or didn't do, Julie couldn't help herself. It wasn't her fault that she got sick, that her fever spiked so high it did permanent damage to her brain."

Lamont sat across from Adam. "Your mom's right, son. Julie is mentally ill. I know it's hard to wrap your mind around it, but it took a lot of love for her to do what she did."

"Empty our bank accounts to pay for her medications? Why didn't she just *tell* me she had a problem? That's what our *insurance* was for!"

"Try to see it from her point of view, honey," Nadine said. "Julie wasn't capable of rational thinking. Because of her sickness, she believed she could pull off the charade, and because of the sickness, she convinced herself it was the only way to hold on to you."

"Maybe," he said. Then he shook his head. "I don't know. I just don't know."

No one spoke for a long time. Finally, Adam broke the sad, strained silence. "Remind me, how old was Julie when they diagnosed her?"

"Between fourteen and fifteen," Lamont said.

He faced Nadine. "You don't think. It's not possible, is it, that… I mean, can the docs do tests, find out if Amy—"

"Adam," Lamont interrupted, a hand on the younger man's forearm, "the damage to Julie's brain was the result of a fever—a very high fever that lasted nearly a week. Schizophrenia isn't in Amy's DNA."

Scrubbing both hands over his face, Adam said, "Well, thank God for that, at least."

The grandfather clock in the hall gonged, announcing the half hour. Nine-thirty? Sure seemed later, Nadine thought. Much later than that.

She'd sat quietly, trying to absorb everything Lamont had said about Julie and her history. Like Adam, she'd slowly paged through the file as he spoke. For most of the time the folder sat on her lap, the words typed and written by the experts blurred before her eyes. The girl's peculiar family history—the illness that caused her problems, diagnoses and descriptions of behavior patterns, medications and dosages, psychiatric definitions—raised more questions than answers. And when everything had been said, they still had nothing that might lead them to Julie's whereabouts.

"If it's okay with you guys, I'm going upstairs." Standing, he bent to pick up the folder. "Mind if I take this with me?"

Nodding, Lamont said, "Not at all. But before you head up, how 'bout we pray together?"

Still holding the file, Adam sat beside Nadine. "Thanks for this, Lamont."

He shrugged. "I only wish it had been more helpful."

"It gave us more than we had."

The threesome bowed their heads and closed their eyes as Lamont said, "Dear Heavenly Father, we thank you for the blessings You've provided, even during these trying times. We ask that you watch over Julie. Keep her safe until she's back in the loving arms of her family. Touch her heart, Lord, and remind her that her husband and little girl need her to come home soon.

"Bless this young man, Lord, and turn his confusion and anger into forgiveness and acceptance. Grant him the strength to fulfill his marriage vows, so that when his young wife returns to him, he can truly live the words *in sickness and in health*. Let him become the earthly source of strength and support she so desperately needs.

"And bless this woman before you, dear God, whose life has been more upside down than rightside up lately. Give her the courage she'll need to get through these next harrowing days, while the authorities unearth proof that she is innocent of all wrongdoing.

"As for this man, Lord, grant me the wisdom to know what to say and when to say it, what to do and what not to do, for these, Your devoted followers. In Your most holy name, we ask these things…

"Amen," they said together.

Nadine's tears didn't surprise her, for she often cried while praying. Under circumstances like these, the shimmer in her son's eyes was predictable, too. But when she looked across the small space that separated her from Lamont, and saw that his gray eyes glistened with unshed tears, Nadine knew without question that this was the man God wanted her to spend the rest of her life with.

Adam gave her a sideways hug, rousing her from her reverie. "You're the best, Mom. I love you," he said before standing.

Lamont got to his feet, too, and wrapped the younger man in a fatherly embrace. Without words, he conveyed that Adam was loved and accepted, that he could count on Lamont to do anything possible to help put things right.

Unable to speak, Adam merely nodded and left the room.

Once he was out of earshot, Nadine said, "What a beautiful, meaningful prayer. Thank you, for that, and for everything."

"Darlin'," he said, "I only wish I had the power to make the whole mess go away."

"I know." And she did, too. "Hungry?"

"You know me." He patted his thigh. "Hollow leg." Grinning, he added, "What do you have in mind?"

"How's a root beer float sound?"

"Can't remember the last time I had one."

"Six years ago, at the twenty-fifth anniversary of our church, when I ran the ice cream bar." She grabbed his hand, led him to the kitchen. "You had a root beer float, a hot fudge sundae and a banana split."

"You remember what I ate *six years ago?*" He chuckled. "If I had a lick of sense, I'd ask you to marry me, right here and now."

She might have said, "Go ahead, ask me," if Amy hadn't run into the room, blond pigtails askew and pajama top untucked from its matching bottom.

"Something is wrong with Obnoxious!" she blubbered. "He's breathing funny and he can't stand up."

"Thanks for opening the office at this hour, Doc."

"Happy to do it," the vet said, leading them to an exam room. "So why do you think it's rat poison?"

"Drooling, muscle tremors, can't stand. As I told you on the phone," Nadine said.

Meb Stone pressed a stethoscope to the dog's underbelly. "Any idea how much he ingested?"

"No," Lamont answered. "Frankly, I can't figure out how he got into the stuff in the first place. I've always kept it in the shed, under lock and key."

Scribbling notes on his clipboard, Stone frowned.

"Maybe he wandered off the ranch, got into something on somebody else's property?"

"I suppose that's possible," Nadine said, remembering that a day earlier, she'd scolded him for tracking bloody fur into the kitchen. "Obviously, some sort of rodent ate the poison and poor Obnoxious ate the rodent."

At the sound of her voice, Obnoxious raised his head and whimpered. Instantly, she was at his side, stroking his head and uttering soothing words.

Meb winked at Nadine. "Think you can stomach what comes next?"

"If I can't, all those summers I worked for you were a complete waste."

"Of your time and mine," the vet agreed, grinning. "I'll need to get him on an IV, for starters, take some blood tests... But you know the drill."

Lamont could birth a foal while blindfolded, and had successfully helped dozens of cows deliver breach calves. While his girls were small, he'd bandaged countless skinned knees and elbows, tended more cases of poison ivy than he cared to count, all without incident. But seeing his beloved dog in this condition set his nerves to jangling.

As Nadine got the IV drip going, Lamont counted yet another reason to admire her. She'd never mentioned having worked for Doc Stone. He could almost picture how she'd react when he mentioned it later. "No big deal," she'd say with a smile and a shrug. And she'd mean every word.

Lamont stood slack-jawed with amazement as she calmly and deftly inserted a needle, then withdrew several vials of blood. After labeling and setting each one aside, she took Obnoxious's temperature. It wasn't until she pulled a clear-plastic hose from storage cabinet that Lamont flinched. "What's that for?"

"Sorry," she started, a look of pity on her gorgeous face, "but we need to induce vomiting. Rat poison thins the blood, so if we don't—"

"No need to explain. I trust you." Evidently, so did Obnoxious who, though he hadn't been anesthetized, lay perfectly still. "He'll be okay, right, Doc?"

"From the looks of things, I'd say you got him here in the nick of time."

"He'll need to go easy for a couple days," Nadine said. "No food for a day or two, then soft stuff."

"If he makes it, y'mean," Lamont put in.

Tilting her head, she narrowed her eyes. "He's a big, strong dog who loves his life. He'll make it." Bending, she kissed the white streak on the dog's black forehead. "Right, boy?"

Obnoxious made a feeble attempt to lick her

cheek, issued a weak whimper and laid his head back down.

Lamont sat on a tall stool in the corner, watching and praying. If anything happened to Obnoxious, well, life at River Valley just wouldn't be the same without him. The thought conjured an image of Amy, red-eyed and sniffling as she clung to her daddy's pants leg when Nadine and Lamont left for the veterinary clinic. She loved that dog almost as much as he did. And in the months she'd been with him, Nadine had grown mighty attached to the goofy mutt, too.

Could they handle yet another loss?

Hopefully, they'd never have to find out.

Chapter Thirteen

"Where's Obnoxious?" Amy demanded the minute they walked in the door.

Hadn't the poor kid been through enough, he wondered, without having to cope with this, too? Lamont bolted the door as Nadine hugged her. "He's doing great," she said, brushing blond bangs from the child's face. "Doc Stone wants to him to stay at the clinic for a couple of days, to keep an eye on him."

The girl rubbed sleepy eyes. "Can I go see him?"

"Tomorrow, maybe," Nadine told her, "if Doc Stone says it's okay."

Adam lifted Amy in his arms. "Time for you to hit the hay, peanut," he said, kissing her cheek.

"Time for you to take your own good advice," Lamont said. "You look like you've been run over by a Mack truck."

"Yeah, that's about how I feel, too." He headed for the staircase, stopping on the landing. "Glad Obnoxious is gonna be okay."

The grandfather clock gonged once as Adam disappeared around the corner.

"If we're going to get any sleep at all tonight, maybe I should make us a nice big mug of warm milk."

Lamont grimaced. "Ack. I'd rather stay up all night."

"Hot tea, then?"

"How 'bout I brew us a pot of decaf coffee, and maybe while it's perking, we'll get sleepy all on our own."

Her expression said what words needn't: "It's worth a try, I suppose."

The fluorescent bulb in the stove hood bathed the room with an opalescent glow. He tried to concentrate on the task at hand—filling the carafe with water, shoving a filter into the pot's basket, counting out three scoops of grounds—but Nadine's blond waves sparkled like spun honey and her eyes shimmered like blue diamonds. He'd made a decision earlier, and if he could muster the nerve, he'd carry it out, right now.

"I saved us the last two slices of chocolate cake."

"Kinda cancels out the decaf, but I'm game if you are."

Nadine knew exactly how he liked the table set, with utensils and napkin to the left of the plate, mug at twelve o'clock. A small thing, really, but it mattered. A lot. And the fact that it did bolstered his courage.

She opened the freezer. "Ice cream with your cake?"

"I declare, woman, either you're trying to make me fat, or—"

She laughed. "As hard as you work around here? You'd need to consume ten thousand calories a day to gain an ounce!"

When she flicked the coffeemaker's on switch, he wrapped a hand around her slender wrist and pulled her to him.

"Lamont, I'm trying to—"

"I know what you're trying to do," he interrupted as she struggled against him, "you're trying to drive me crazy." Now he wrapped both arms around her. "How do you expect me to react when you stand there, looking all gorgeous, saying and doing sweet things for me?"

She didn't react, except to stop squirming.

"I've made a habit of holding on to something that's gone," he said, "and—"

"Rose will never really be gone," Nadine said,

pressing a hand to his chest, "as long as she's *here*." She touched a finger to his temple. "And here. I think it's a wonderful, beautiful thing, the way you love her still."

Clearly, he wasn't getting through to her. Somehow, she'd gotten the impression that he was still *in love with* Rose, and that he was trying to excuse and explain the way he'd clung to her memory.

But she couldn't be further from the truth. Lamont led her to the nearest chair. "Have a seat," he instructed, and when she opened her mouth to protest, he held up a hand. "Bear with me, okay?"

Bobbing her head, she huffed quietly and plopped onto the cushion.

"I realized something tonight, standing up there in my room, surrounded by decades worth of old photographs—"

Tears shimmered in her eyes when she said, "If my marriage to Ernest had been *half* what yours and Rose's was, well, you should *never* feel the need to apologize for your loyalty to her. Any woman who'd let a thing like that upset her isn't worth your time."

In other words, he thought, smiling, *she* would never begrudge him fond memories of his wife. Gently, he chucked her chin. "Nadine, darlin', will you please let me finish?" He cleared his throat.

"As I was *saying,* I've lived in the past for so long that I almost forgot about the present. And the future." He got onto one knee in front of her chair, both hands gripping her slender waist. "I loved Rose more than life itself, and sometimes…"

The apprehensive look on her face silenced him, threatening not only to destroy his optimistic mood, but his courage as well. Right before coming downstairs, he'd put the ring into his jeans pocket. Then, as now, he hoped for a moment like this, when he could confess that she was the answer to his prayers.

"The coffee's done," she said, trying to wriggle free of his embrace.

"Not so fast. I've got something to say, and you're gonna sit there and let me say it."

"But it's late, and we both have to get an early start in the morning."

"Maybe you really *are* trying to drive me crazy!"

"Lamont."

He dug the ring out of his pocket and, holding it between thumb and forefinger, said, "Before she died, my grandmother insisted that love would come knocking again." He turned the ring left, then right. "So what do you say?"

She sat for what seemed like an eternity, blinking and staring at the gold band. Lamont thanked

God he couldn't read her mind, because he had a feeling he wouldn't like what was going on in that pretty head of hers—not one bit.

"You're kidding, right?"

"Never been more serious in my life."

"Who designed it?"

What an odd question, he thought, especially at a moment like this. "Grandma always said Grandpa had a poet's soul, so I guess he gets all the credit."

Her face went dreamy and her voice got soft as she said, "What does the inscription say?"

"See for yourself."

"'Two are better than one.' From Ecclesiastes." She handed it back. "It's beautiful. And the diamonds? What do they signify?"

"Faith, hope and love."

She nodded somberly. "That's what I thought."

This wasn't going the way he'd hoped it would. Not even close. "Put me out of my misery, and say yes, will you?"

She scooted to the edge of the chair and sat up straight. "I can't."

He ran his free hand through his hair. This didn't make sense! She'd shown him in every way possible that she loved him. "Why *not?*"

"There are a hundred reasons."

That hurt more than he cared to admit. "Really," he said, moving to his own chair. "That many."

She got up, filled two mugs with coffee and carried them both to the table. They sat quietly for a few minutes, sipping coffee and poking at their cake before she broke the tense silence. "With everything that's going on—Julie missing and Obnoxious in the clinic and the arson charges hanging over my head—I can't in good conscience burden you with all that. I mean, I know you're sort of stuck with it, since we've been mooching off you for so long. But that's different from being officially and permanently saddled down by it all."

He shoved the cake plate away, let his fork clatter to the tabletop. "Never figured you for a hypocrite, Nadine."

Eyes wide, her eyebrows disappeared beneath her bangs. "A *hypocrite!*"

"All your praying and churchgoing and talk of miracles and God and faith. Where's all that, huh? Why can't you *believe* that tomorrow Obnoxious will be home, dogging everybody's heels, and Julie will turn up, and when she does, we'll get her the help she needs. Why can't you accept there's no way they can hang that arson charge on you, and *believe* in your own innocence, the way I do?"

He couldn't seem to stop himself. Didn't *want* to stop himself because, God forgive him, he wanted her to hurt as much as she'd hurt him. "What's wrong with you that you don't want to be happy?"

She stared at him for a brittle moment. "I want to be happy," she said, putting the ring on the table, "but I can't…no, I won't take my happiness at your expense." With that, she got to her feet and strode purposefully toward the door. "Just leave those dishes where they are," she said over her shoulder. "I'll take care of them in the morning."

Lamont heard the creak in the upstairs hall, and it told him that Nadine had already ducked into her room. The grandfather clock gonged, telling him it was 2:00 a.m.

And the diamond-studded band that winked up at him from the table told him his heart was breaking, even before tears stung his eyes.

During the next few agonizing days, Lamont found plenty of excuses to stay out of the house. On the rare occasions when he ran into Nadine, he could barely look at her. He felt like an idiot. And a fool. Because he'd put it all out there, and she'd rejected him. Only losing Rose had hurt as much.

Maybe what he needed was time to himself, in a place where he was sure not to run into her. It had been a while since he'd restocked the bunkhouse. It was as good an excuse to hide out as any.

Miles from the nearest road, the little shack had provided safe haven for many a River Valley ranch hand—and their boss, on occasion—looking to escape the bitter winds of a blizzard or the blinding grit of a dust storm.

He had taken each of his daughters there on their thirteenth birthdays. The first few days, he stayed with them, teaching them how to take care of themselves in the event that they ever got stranded on the prairie. And then he'd left them on their own for a night—or so they thought— bunking down in the back of his pickup half a mile up the road, where he could watch and listen and get to them if anything went wrong. To give them their due, all four girls had stuck it out, and all four of them had thanked him in the ensuing years, for giving them an experience that bolstered their self-confidence. All four had returned from time to time, to cram for exams or heal from a broken heart, always coming home more self-assured than when they'd left.

He'd done what he could to make the place as comfortable as possible, though he refused to run electricity or water to it. Not because of the cost in dollars and energy, but because he liked having a place to go where he could get a sense for what life had been like for his father and grandfather, making it on their own in the middle of nowhere. If he hadn't had the girls to take care of, he probably would have moved out there after Rose's death…and stayed.

He hiked to the equipment shed that housed tractors and old pickups used for moving hay or hauling trash to the road, and saw that his old red truck wasn't in its usual place. He figured the ranch hands he'd sent to town for rope and saddle wax had taken it. Odd, considering they could have chosen newer, easier-riding vehicles.

Checking the row of hooks on the wall, he chose the keys to his favorite truck. The motor turned over on the very first crank. Maybe he'd bring Frank out here, let him see how *this* '65 Chevy purred, Lamont thought, grinning.

In no time, the bed creaked under the weight of dry and canned goods. If the Canadian River was running, a stranded cowboy—or London daughter—could dip water from its banks and, with a fire in the belly of the woodstove, rustle up a rib-stickin' meal. But since the construction of several dams upriver, it was more likely that the dry Texas winds had lapped every drop from her banks. Much as Lamont detested the tasteless stuff, he added bottled water to the truck.

He tossed in a metal canister of kitchen matches

to light the oil lanterns when night fell. Clean sheets and blankets, secured in plastic bins, would offer comfort to the dog-tired few who find themselves in a position of having to spend a night or two on one of the crude wooden cots. A new first aid kit rounded out his list and, after parking the loaded truck near the back door, he headed for bed.

Lamont tossed and turned, unable to sleep. He didn't know which to blame—the fact that Nadine had not agreed to become his wife, or anticipation about visiting the bunkhouse after so many months. Before the sun peeked over the horizon, he found himself heading north, alternately sipping hot black coffee from a Thermos and munching on a cold toaster tart.

He caught himself smiling when the building finally came into view. Silhouetted against the red-streaked morning sky, it sat squat and wide, with nothing but a dozen scraggly salt cedar trees and scrubby shrubs serving as a backdrop. As he got closer, Lamont noticed that the wild grasses had been flattened into two distinct tracks. Tires had caused the paths, and recently, too.

Didn't seem likely that a drifter had bedded down in the cabin, because the place sat back too far to be seen from the road. Odder still, the door stood slightly ajar. No Texan in his right mind would have done that, for it was a sure way to invite diamondbacks, scorpions and pine caterpillars in out of the sun. Scowling, he made a mental note find out which of the knuckleheads on his payroll had been so careless, and went inside to inspect the usual nooks and crannies. Though the place was critter-free, something seemed off. For starters, it was way too early in the day to be this hot in the bunkhouse.

Just as he'd suspected, Lamont found glowing coals in the belly of the woodstove. The scent of boiled coffee clung to the dry, dusty air, and a soiled crockery bowl sat beside a still-warm pot of stew. An indentation in a bed pillow caught his eye, reminding Lamont that he'd read *The Three Bears* to Amy last evening. Suddenly, he empathized with Papa Bear. Somebody had been sleeping in his bed.

Julie came instantly to mind. What if she'd decided that all she and her young, angry husband needed was some time apart? That's what had brought Lamont here, after all. And he'd given her free rein of the place. What would have stopped her from borrowing his red truck?

But if she had, where was it?

Peering out each window, Lamont scanned the horizon, hoping for a glimpse of it. Plenty of ways to hide a vehicle out here, if a body had a mind to.

As he off-loaded the supplies, Lamont wondered how she'd survived the days, all by herself, with no money, no running water, no plumbing and no electricity? And if a seasoned cowboy like himself sometimes found nights on the prairie cold and daunting, how had a city girl held out this long? "That'll teach you not to judge a book by its cover," he muttered, sliding behind the steering wheel.

Suddenly, Lamont's neck hairs bristled, exactly as they had on a similar morning, years earlier, when he'd ridden out to the north pasture to check on a wintering herd. He looked up just in time to spot a mountain lion, perched on the rocky outcropping above him, ready to spring. To this day, he didn't know which saved his hide, the single shot fired into the air to spook the cat, or that eerie "Somebody's watching" sensation.

He steered the truck over the rocky, rutted road. With every glance in the rearview mirror, Lamont hoped for a glimpse of Julie, or whoever had camped out in the bunkhouse. If he saw her, he'd make sure she understood how worried and distraught they'd all been since finding her note. Maybe, knowing how much she was loved and missed, the girl would swallow her pride and let him take her home without making a fuss.

Not likely, given her medical history, but that didn't stop him from praying for it, anyway.

He hesitated before turning onto the highway, took one last, long look behind him. But Lamont saw nothing but scrubby pines and knee-high weeds, and prayed the good Lord would look out for the confused young woman who hid among them.

Chapter Fourteen

He found the private detective sitting at his piled-high desk, tapping an eraserless pencil on his forehead. Without looking up from the folder on his blotter, he drawled, "Been expecting you, London."

"Why, 'cause I called and said I was coming?" Grinning, Lamont helped Winston find a new napping place. And as the tabby curled up on the makeshift credenza, he added, "New case?"

"Nope, yours." Leaning back, Frank clasped both hands behind his head. *"Still."*

Chuckling, Lamont sat in the cat-warmed chair. "Good gravy. I'll have to sell a hundred acres to pay your bill." He nodded at the file. "So what's new?"

"If the fire marshal doesn't charge your girl-friend's daughter-in-law with that fire, I'll eat my hat." He held up a hand to silence Lamont's retort.

"I know, I know. I've said that before. But I'm 100 percent sure about this. So sure that if I'm wrong, I won't just eat *my* hat, I'll eat yours, too."

It had been painful, admitting to himself that Nadine wanted nothing more than friendship from him. How much more would it hurt, he wondered, saying it out loud?

Instead, Lamont launched into the story of how, after his trip to the bunkhouse, he and Adam and half a dozen ranch hands fanned out on horseback, searching every acre for miles for a sign of the girl. After three days without so much as a boot-print, they concluded it had been a vagrant, and not Julie, who'd holed up in the cabin.

After popping a chocolate kiss into his mouth, Frank rolled the foil into a tiny silver ball and tossed it from palm to palm. "If I'd burnt down my mother-in-law's house, guess I'd run off, too. Can't say I blame the li'l fruitcake."

Lamont winced. "Isn't Julie's fault that she's—"

"A bubble off plumb? Off her nut? Crazy as a loon? Wacky as a—"

"Enough. Adam wants to meet you," he said, changing the subject, "the sooner the better."

Frank faced his computer monitor, and a flurry of keystrokes brought his calendar to the screen. "How's three o'clock?"

"Sounds good, but let me check, just to be sure."

Sliding his cell phone from his pocket, Lamont dialed home. When Nadine picked up, his heart skipped a beat. And ached. A strange and foolish and stupid reaction, because she'd been lady of the house for months now. Who else would answer his phone?

"He's in the barn," she said when he asked for her son. "Want me to get him?"

"Nah. Don't waste time, running back and forth. Just grab a pencil…" He rattled off Frank's phone number and directions to his office. "Tell Adam I'll meet him here."

"Has Frank learned anything more about Julie?"

He heard the tentative note in her voice, but no way he intended to shoulder the burden of guilt over it. She'd made the decision to reject *him,* not the other way around. "Not really."

He listened to her impatient sigh, and though he tried to fight it, it cut him to the quick.

"Will you be home for supper?"

It was the sort of question a wife might ask a husband who called home from work during a routine coffee break. Maybe *she* could pretend things were fine between them, but he sure didn't know how to. "Dunno," he grumbled. "Depends on traffic, I guess."

"Oh. Right. I'd almost forgotten how awful rush hour can be."

Okay, now she sounded out-and-out hurt, and

yes, he felt like a lout, knowing his gruff manner had caused it. But for the love of God, what did she expect? She'd built a thick, high wall between them. Did she expect him to stay on his own side of it, and enjoy being there, too?

"Drive safely, okay?"

"Will do," he said, and snapped the phone shut.

As he dropped it into his shirt pocket, Frank chuckled. "Trouble in paradise?"

Lamont only stared, inspiring a nonchalant shrug from Frank. "To be fair, I only heard half of that conversation—though it's a stretch to call it a 'conversation'—but things sounded pretty tense to me."

Leaning forward, he spoke slowly, quietly. "Frank, you 'n' me—we go way back. I like you. Always have. Respect the work you do, too. If you ever need a hand, you know I'm your man." He narrowed his eyes. "But what goes on under my roof is none of your business. Got it?"

"Has this mess you got yourself into really turned you so old and crotchety that you can't take a joke any more?"

"Say something funny," Lamont said, "and I'll laugh with the best of 'em."

Frank considered that for a moment. "Fair enough."

"Do me a favor and keep your references to nutjobs and loony tunes to yourself when Adam gets here. The kid's already been through the wringer."

"Fair enough," Frank repeated. And glancing at his watch, closed Lamont's file. "How 'bout I buy you lunch, bring you up to speed on the latest Julie findings."

"Is your calendar still open on that gizmo of yours?"

Both brows drew together in the center of Frank's forehead. "Sorry, pal, I'm not following."

"Just thought it'd be a good idea to make an official record of it." One forefinger scribbled in the air, "Frank Duvall Opens Wallet."

Grabbing a Rangers baseball cap from the inside doorknob, Frank chuckled. "Let's hope River Valley never goes belly-up."

"Why?"

"Because you'll never make a living as a stand-up comic."

Sometimes, Nadine thought, lying awake for the umpteenth night in a row, having a conscience wasn't necessarily a good thing. If not for her acute sense of right and wrong, she might have been able to pretend she hadn't hurt Lamont.

In the years since Ernest's death, Nadine worked hard to shed the "damsel in distress" cloak that made her susceptible to his empty promises. As she grew more independent, self-sufficiency allowed her to see herself as a clear-thinking, feet-on-the-ground sort of woman.

Cold reality squeezed around her heart as she admitted that she'd been lying to herself.

Just as Ernest had vowed to take her away from her abusive, alcoholic father, Lamont had come to her rescue, saving her and the kids from bankruptcy and homelessness. Would he subject her to physical and emotional abuse, as her husband had? Not likely, but since no one could offer a guarantee, Nadine couldn't risk it. *Wouldn't* risk it.

She'd carry the guilt of having accepted his generosity and kindness, of leading him to believe in their love—*if* that's what this was—until her dying breath. It was her fault, and hers alone, that they'd both suffer the heartache and humiliation of a separation when she got out on her own again, because, just as with Ernest, she'd leaped into the arms of the first hero to come along… without praying for the Lord's guidance. Physical scars were the here-and-now evidence of her lack of common sense back then. And this time, her heart and soul—and Lamont's—would bear the wounds of her foolishness.

Nadine had kept herself deliberately busy and, thankfully, so had Lamont, because how could she look him in the eye after taking so much from him and giving him nothing but grief and pain in return? He'd done more—so much more—than open his house to her and the kids. And how had she repaid him? By making him feel like a stranger in his own home. If a more vile and contemptible woman existed, she certainly didn't want to meet her.

She had to concentrate on the fact that he was strong of character. It would sting for a while but, in time, his wounded ego and hurt feelings would heal. No way that could happen if she let him put that ring on her finger. "You're doing this for his own good" had become her mantra, and if it took a hundred years to believe it in her heart, she'd keep right on telling herself that.

Now, as thunder shook the house and lightning flashed outside the windows, she bit back tears. How unjust it seemed that, despite what he no doubt saw as a heartless, careless rebuff, *she* still had a safe place to call home, while Julie—whose offenses had been unintentional—was out there somewhere, cold and alone and afraid. If she could trade places with the girl, she'd do it in the blink of an eye. Maybe that would put the scales of justice into better balance.

"What's up?"

Thankfully, she was facing the sink when Adam

entered the kitchen. She couldn't bear to disappoint him, too, by letting him witness her teary, self-centered weakness. "Just fixing a light supper, that's all."

He distributed the plates and utensils she'd set out earlier. "All right, out with it."

"Out with what?" she asked, putting the soup pot onto a trivet.

"You were chompin' at the bit before to put in your two cents when Lamont and I told you what Frank said."

He was referring to what the salesman had told the reporter. "I'm worried about how she'll feel about all of us, after she comes home, I mean. I didn't exactly do a good job of bolstering her ego when I found out about the missing money."

"None of this is your fault, Mom," he said, gripping the back of the nearest chair. "I know I didn't confide much in you after Julie and I were married, but…" He paused, hung his head, as if struggling to find the right words. "You're not easy act to follow, you know, with your 'can-do' attitude. I was stupid—and mean—comparing her to you. If I hadn't wasted so much time pretending things were fine, maybe I'd have taken her to get some help. Because there were signs. Lots of them."

"What kind of signs?"

He shrugged. "She thought everybody was out

to get her all the time. You should've heard some of the stuff she'd say about those gals she worked with."

"But honey, she's young. And inexperienced. We all have to live a little before we can tell the difference between a friend and a—"

"No, this was different, as if she actually believed people were out to destroy her. Or worse. There were times when she literally pulled her hair out, worrying about it."

Nadine tried to imagine what that must have been like for Julie. Marriage to Ernest hadn't been easy, but even at its worst, it hadn't made her question her sanity.

"She even thought maybe you wanted to get rid of her."

A hand over her heart, Nadine gasped. "What! But I couldn't have loved her more if she'd been my very own."

"I know that. And I tried to convince *her* of that." Again, he shook his head. "When all that money went missing, she convinced herself that you didn't trust her—or even like her any more."

"How could I have been so blind! If only I'd spent more time with her, shown her more affection, instead of being all wrapped up in my own petty prob—"

"I've been reading up on her condition, and even

when schizophrenics are off their drugs, they can sometimes see the real world for what it is. She made some stupid decisions, and we might never know why—or understand them—but they were *her* choices, and I think somewhere in that fuzzy world where she lives, she knew that. I think *that's* what made her run away."

Her heart ached for Adam. If only she had it within her power to ease his suffering, to erase his guilt. Nadine was proud, too, of the strong, loving young man he'd become. She hugged him, then ruffled his hair, the way she had when he was a boy. "God will help us," was all she could think to say. "When Julie comes home, He'll show us what she needs and make sure we have the strength to give it to her."

"I want to believe that, Mom. More than anything."

After breakfast the following morning, Nadine made a beeline for the toolshed. If she waited just one more day to clean up after Obnoxious, the yard would never recover.

"Now where do you suppose Julie put that shovel?" she wondered aloud.

And then she saw that it had slipped from its hook, its handle keeping the low, swing-away window from closing all the way. The dirt floor was covered with tracks and droppings, and she pitied the poor jackrabbit that had hopped inside and gobbled its fill of rat poison. Now she understood how Obnoxious had come by his bloodied muzzle the day before his near-death experience. Tonight, they'd give thanks for his complete recovery with a pot roast and all the trimmings, and the big goofy hound would get his share, too.

But with no word about Julie's whereabouts, no one felt much like celebrating. Nadine was dishing up wedges of home-baked chocolate cake when the phone rang.

"I'll get it," Lamont said.

He carried the portable phone from the kitchen, muttering and mumbling under his breath for a good five minutes.

"Was it Mommy?" Amy asked when he returned.

Lamont bent to kiss the top of her head, then took his place at the head of the table. "No, sweet girl, I'm afraid not."

"Frank?" Adam asked.

Nodding, Lamont absentmindedly painted his plate with fudge frosting. "It was mostly good news." He took a swallow of milk, and with a nod toward Amy, implied he'd deliver the not-so-good news later.

Nadine could almost hear the disappointment

draining from her son as Lamont sent her a sad half smile.

"Seems ol' Frank's puppy-to-the-root tendencies have paid off." He went on to explain how the detective had stubbornly refused to accept Marcus's findings, and hired two separate fire investigation specialists. Both came back with the same results: What had appeared to be gasoline, deliberately spattered onto the walls and floor, was instead the contents of the oil lantern that had always stood on an end table in Nadine's parlor. Claw marks on what remained of the window trim indicated that to access her favorite perch on the wide sill, Julie's cat, Peeper, had upset the table, overturning the lamp.

So that's what Julie was trying to tell me the night I cut my hand in the dishwater.

"Frank said to tell you to expect a call from Marcus."

Adam put his fork down and shoved back from the table. "You mean they're dropping the arson charges?"

"Yup."

Lamont's quiet tone told her what words needn't: He understood that now the insurance company could write a check, freeing Nadine to study floor plans and choose the colors and materials that would become her home. In time, he'd realize how much better off he'd be once she was out of his house and on her own again. And God willing, with a little distance between them, maybe they could reestablish the once-companionable nature of their relationship, because if not, oh, how she'd miss him!

"Guess I'll get Amy tucked in," Adam said, hoisting her from her chair.

"Will you read me two stories, Daddy?"

"You know I will." He kissed both chubby cheeks and shot a quick glance at Lamont. "It'll only take fifteen or twenty minutes."

On his feet now, Lamont nodded. "I'll be in my office." He leaned in to pop a kiss on Amy's up-turned nose. "Sweet dreams, baby duck. See you in the morning."

The child climbed from her dad's arms to Lamont's with the ease and speed of a chimp, and pressed both chubby palms to his cheeks. "I love you *sooo* much, Unka Lamont!" Then she hugged him long and hard and climbed back into Adam's arms.

Nadine followed them to the bottom of the stairway. "Soon as I get the dishes cleaned up, I'll come in to give you a good-night kiss."

The dishes could wait, she decided as she hurried back to the kitchen, until after she thanked Lamont.

The good news from Frank wouldn't have been possible if he hadn't funded the investigation.

Her heart sank when she heard Lamont's office door close at the other end of the hall. Obnoxious trotted up and sat, waiting for a pat on the head. "You're a handsome old boy," she said, bending to scratch his forehead, "but much as it pains me to say it, you're a sorry second to your master."

The dog whimpered and snuggled closer, and as she hugged his furry neck, Nadine knew it would be a long, lonely night.

A bittersweet feeling enveloped Nadine as she went about her chores the next day. Relief that she'd been cleared of the ugly accusations was diminished by the knowledge that she'd hurt Lamont by turning down his proposal. Guilt and regret churned in her veins as she prayed for a way to show him how much he meant to her, how grateful she was for all he'd so selflessly done for her and the kids.

And then while gathering eggs from her henhouse, an idea dawned.

For the first time in months, hope and happiness glowed inside her as she prepared dinner for the ranch hands. Lamont's crew put in long hours and required plenty of substantial food at the midday meal. That meant filling dozens of bowls with nourishing yet palate-satisfying foods like beans, mashed potatoes and gravy, oven-fried chicken and hearty biscuits. They ate it with gusto, barely leaving enough to scrape into Obnoxious's bowl.

As much as she enjoyed watching them devour every morsel, she enjoyed the calm and quiet mood of the evening meal even more, when it was just Lamont, Adam and Amy and herself. She liked this early-fall time of year, too, when twilight came early, suffusing the house with a slower, easier pace than the one that characterized the bright light of day.

While Adam and Lamont ate and discussed the next day's chores, Amy chattered happily, inspiring Nadine to thank God for blessing little children with such amazing coping skills. Between bites of grilled cheese and sips of tomato soup, the child seemed content to remain in Lamont's homey kitchen forever. Questions about where her mommy had gone and when she'd come home dwindled from dozens a day to a mere one or two, usually at bedtime. Nadine didn't know which made her sadder, the child who used to miss her mother so much that she cried herself to sleep every night, or the one who seemed to have adapted to a life without constant pressure and strife.

"I smell smoke," Amy said around a mouthful of macaroni and cheese.

As Nadine looked behind her to make sure all the burners had been turned off, Adam said, "She's right. I smell something, too."

Lamont sniffed his way to the French doors that led to the terrace and the outbuildings beyond. "It's coming from—"

Adam hollered, "The barn's on fire!"

Instantly, Nadine was on her feet.

"Call the fire department," Lamont ordered, "while Adam and I check things out."

They raced out the door and across the back lawn so quickly that they probably hadn't heard her say, "Please be careful!"

By now the whinnying of the frightened horses had reached the house, too. "Oh, Grandmom," Amy said, staring wide-eyed and terrified out the window, "they won't die, will they?"

She grabbed the phone and dialed 911, then gave her granddaughter's slender shoulder a gentle squeeze. "Your daddy and Uncle Lamont will do everything they can to save them."

When the operator answered, Nadine spelled out the problem and provided the address. Would the woman realize that the department had been summoned to another fire, right up the road?

She hung up feeling feeble and frail, because there wasn't a blessed thing she could do to help Lamont and Adam move the horses from the barn to the corral. And what about poor old Obnoxious, who paced and huffed puny warning barks to anyone who might threaten his home and family?

She dropped to her knees, and, hugging Amy tight, began reciting the Twenty-Third Psalm. Because despite feeling helpless and powerless, she believed He would see them through this, just as He'd seen them through every other tragedy that had befallen them. She had faith that He'd bring Lamont and Adam back to her, safe and sound, because if anything happened to either of them, Nadine didn't think she could trust Him, ever again.

Chapter Fifteen

Lamont knew better than to focus on the terrified trumpeting of the horses. Instead, he directed Adam's actions until they performed like a well-seasoned team. It seemed to take forever to lead the agitated animals into the corral, but by the time they'd latched the gate securely behind them, two fire engines had roared up the drive, sirens screaming and lights flashing.

In the wraithlike, bloody glow of the fire's light, Adam's looked much older than his years. Did the boy share Lamont's concerns that Julie might somehow be responsible for this fire? The younger man answered the unasked question with one of his own: "Can I have the keys to your gun cabinet?"

He studied the boy's eyes, haggard and tired, thanks to the events of the past few weeks. "I'm thinking the Winchester is our best bet."

If Adam hadn't been under such intense pressure, balancing a full-time job and caring for his little girl, all while searching for his missing wife, he never would have considered aiming a loaded weapon at his pretty young wife.

"I think you'll be more useful inside, making sure your mother and daughter stay as far away from this mess as possible."

It took a moment for his words to sink in but, in seconds, Adam nodded. "You're right. Don't know what I was thinking." He turned, as if to go back to the house, but stopped halfway there.

Was it his imagination? The firelight playing tricks on his eyes? Some eerie sort of optical illusion? Or had Adam, too, seen a dark-clothed figure, running duck-and-cover style, beyond the barn?

"Julie!" Adam bellowed, racing toward the spot. "Julie, stop!"

In one instant, the shadowy figure stood stock-still. In the next, it was swallowed up by the dancing light-and-shadow shapes born of the fire.

"Adam," he hollered over the shouts of firefighters, the hiss of water hoses, the rumble of their trucks' engines, "Adam, get back here!"

If the younger man heard him, he made no effort to obey. Before Lamont knew it, the boy had vanished into the blackness. Gone. Out of sight.

"Lord, watch over that hotheaded young fool," he prayed. And even as the words exited his mouth, despite the mayhem and chaos all around him, Lamont knew that in Adam's shoes, he would have done the very same thing.

Marcus strolled up to him, ponderous belly all but covering a shiny Texas-shaped belt buckle. "You people turned into a bunch of pyromaniacs or somethin'?" As if to punctuate his grave statement, the fire marshal walked his toothpick from one side of his mouth to the other. "Did you see something out back earlier?" Marcus asked, calmly wiggling the toothpick between his two front teeth.

"Some*body,* you mean."

"Right. Before Adam took off runnin'."

He nodded.

"Sent two guys over to see what they could shake outta the bushes," he said, frowning at the bent tip of his toothpick. "I oughtn't tell you this," Marcus added, using the toothpick as a pointer, "but I don't believe that li'l gal had anything to do with this. Or the fire at Nadine's, either."

About the time he opened his mouth to ask Marcus on what, if anything, he'd based his observation, a soggy, sooty firefighter ran up.

"Got 'er under control, Marcus." He removed his helmet and skimmed a sooty glove over his brow.

"Good job," he said. And to Lamont, "You'd best put a handful of hunnerts into the collection plate come Sunday, 'cause only thing that explains how quick all this straightened itself out—well, except for this latest mess, anyway—is that you've got the Lord on your side."

Lamont told Marcus the way things had unfolded, leaving out only the part where Adam had asked to fetch the rifle.

"I expect we'll need to talk to you down at the station, but it can wait until tomorrow." He placed a hand on Lamont's shoulder. "For now, go inside and be with your loved ones, and thank the good Lord that He spared y'all again."

Something sinister swirled with the scent of charred wood, and hung in the air like a menacing fog, a solemn oath of impending doom. He watched as the last of Marcus's men climbed aboard the lumbering trucks, and as they ground down the drive, the sensation grew. He needed to find Adam—and find him now.

Lamont gave a thought to heading inside to fetch the Winchester himself, but instead grabbed a coil of rope, hanging from a corral fence post. He slung it over one shoulder and headed to the spot where he'd last seen Adam.

He heard voices, far in the distance. First a woman's, next a man's, soft at first, then growing louder, more agitated with every step he took. Adam had found Julie, and from the sound of things, she was none too happy about it. They faced each other like old West gunslingers. Julie spewed fury like a human volcano, accusing Adam of all manner of vile and despicable things. When she faced Lamont, raw, unbridled disgust beamed from her eyes.

Lamont had heard stories of the Irish banshee, an angry old hag whose face and voice could turn a man's blood to ice. He'd never fully understood how anyone could look or sound so wicked and horrible that they had the power to paralyze humans. He understood now. Understood, too, how in days gone by, people suffering from mental illness were thought to be possessed by the devil himself, because that's exactly how Julie looked to him.

"Julie," he said, taking a step closer, "you don't know how worried we've all been about you. Seeing you, knowing you're all right, it's the answer to our—"

"Shut. Up. You simpering old fool," she spat. "You can't pacify me with lies. I know they say I'm crazy, and maybe I am, but I'm not stupid."

"It's no use, Lamont," Adam said. "She's been off her meds too long. We need to—"

"I won't *go* to another loony bin. *I won't!*" she screamed, running toward the driveway.

Lamont slid the rope from his shoulder, quickly fashioned it into a lasso. In his day, he'd been a better than average wrangler, but it had been a while since he'd roped a calf. "Please God," he said through clenched teeth. "Help me, so we can help *her.*"

The rope rippled out in front of him, rode the smoky, sooty air between him and Julie. If she hadn't turned, seen it hovering above her like a hangman's noose, he'd have caught her, for sure.

But she was young and lithe and light on her feet, and quickly sidestepped the lariat. And then, she was gone.

"Where'd she *go?*" Adam wondered, pivoting.

"Don't know," Lamont said, "but you'd better get back up to the house, because if she gets there first…"

For an instant, a look of dread and terror drained the color from Adam's face, but he quickly regained his composure and raced for the house.

At the first sputtering, grinding sounds of an engine, struggling to come to life, Lamont moved toward the driveway, and saw her rage-twisted face, illuminated by the pickup's dome light, pounding the steering wheel, grimacing as she tested the ignition, over and over.

The scene unfolded before his eyes as if in slow motion.

Tires spewed gravel as they worked to grip the drive.

The truck, speeding full-out toward the highway.

The thundering blast of a big rig's horn.

The high-pitched squeal of tires, skidding on the asphalt.

Metal, crashing into crumpling metal…

And after a millisecond of absolute quiet, the soft tinkling of shattered glass, raining onto the pavement.

The fire trucks had been gone all of five minutes—too long to have heard the crash. So he opened his cell phone, dialed 911 and croaked out the necessary facts that would bring the EMTs up the same driveway that the firefighters had just vacated.

He reached the road just as the trucker leaped down from his cab. The man didn't seem to notice that his mouth and nose were bleeding, that still more of his life's blood oozed from a gash in his forehead. "She pulled right out in front of me," he said, voice trembling. "I jackknifed the rig, trying to stop in time." Both hands pressed to his temples, he hit his knees. "Oh," he moaned. "She ain't dead, is she, mister? Please, God. Tell me she ain't—"

Adam appeared from out of nowhere, silencing the driver. "Stay back, Adam," Lamont barked, holding out an arm out to bar his path. "Let me have a look-see first."

He couldn't say if his hard tone or the sight of the mangled pickup froze the boy in his tracks, but, thankfully Adam, stayed silent and still.

Julie's eyes opened slowly when he walked up to the driver's door. "Guess I…guess I've gone… gone and done it this time," she wheezed.

"Shh," Lamont said, stroking her bloody forehead. "I've called 911. Help's on the way."

"They can't…can't help me."

"You're gonna be fine. Just hush now, and hold my hand until the paramedics get here."

Other than Nadine's, Lamont had never seen bigger, bluer eyes. Julie locked onto his gaze, and when he took hold of her hand, she squeezed it with a power that belied her size and condition.

"Not gonna…can't…make it," came her ragged reply.

"Don't talk like that," he scolded gently. "Don't even *think* it. Listen…hear those sirens?"

Eyes shut now, she gave one weak nod.

Lamont leaned into the truck and, not wanting Adam to hear, whispered hoarsely, "You hold on

Julie Greene. You have a little girl who needs you, and a young husband, too. Both of them love you, so you work hard, you hear? You hang in there and—"

"They don't—" a rumbling wheeze escaped her lungs as a look of agony wrinkled her brow. "—love me. Nobody does. Why would they? I'm…"

Tears stung his eyes as he gave her hand a shake. "They *do* love you. Nadine loves you and I love you. Why, even Peeper and Obnoxious love you!"

That, at least, inspired a tiny smile.

"And God loves you, too."

She studied his face, as if searching for signs of insincerity. "Why?"

It was more a long, jagged breath than a question. "Because you're His little girl, every bit as much as Amy is *your* little girl."

The smile grew by a fraction of an inch, exposing bloodied gums and teeth broken when her face slammed into the steering wheel. "Uh-oh," she rasped, "you're…in trouble, 'cause it's a sin. To tell. A lie…"

"Now you just listen here, young lady—"

Adam ran up and muscled Lamont out of the way. "Julie."

"Hi, honey," she said, "I'm home."

He leaned into the cab and kissed her forehead. "Do you know how to make an entrance, or what?"

She turned to get a better look at his face. "You're not mad at me anymore?"

"Nah. It's history. Over and forgotten."

"Did they...tell you about the oil lamp?"

He nodded. "Yeah. But that's forgotten, too."

Eyes shut tight, she shook her head. "Your mom must hate me."

"No, sweetie. She loves you as much as if you were her own kid. And if she wasn't up at the house, keeping your nosy little girl from running down here to see if her pony survived the fire, she'd tell you that herself."

"I didn't...never meant for the..."

"Julie, honey, for goodness' sake, will you be quiet and save your strength? The ambulance is on its way."

"Don't blame you, not wanting to hear that this fire was an accident, too. And I wouldn't blame you if you didn't believe me. But—"

"If I have to tell you to be quiet one more time, I'll—"

"You'll what," she said, mustering a strength in her voice that belied her condition. "Empty threats. I've got nothing, nothing," she said, and looked away.

"You've got *me*." He kissed her again. "And you've got Amy. *Look* at me, Julie," he said, sobbing now, "You can't leave me. You can't leave Amy. We need you!"

The ambulance came to a screeching halt beside the pickup. One paramedic tended the semi driver while a second quickly set out orange cones to block the road. A third walked up to Adam. "You her husband?"

"Yeah," he said without looking away from Julie. "The paramedics are here, honey, and they're gonna take real good care of you. Now, you fight, you hear me? Fight like you never fought before. Do it for Amy and me!"

"All right. I'll try."

"Do or do not," he said, quoting the old movie line, "there *is* no try!"

"Okay, Adam. Okay..."

Lamont's heart ached for the boy. Adam looked as helpless as he'd felt on half a dozen occasions in his life. Like the night his own wife had died in an accident much like this one, and the night Cammi told him that she'd eloped with some loser who'd gotten himself killed—in an accident much like this one.

He'd draw on his own experience to help the boy.

He'd pray that Julie would make it.

Pray that if she didn't, Adam wouldn't waste precious time wallowing in self-pity, because Amy would need him, just as his own girls had needed him after they'd buried Rose.

Prayed the Lord would see fit to grace him with the words this poor kid so desperately needed to hear, no matter how things turned out.

He walked slowly toward Adam and held out his arms. And there, in the red-and-blue strobes of the ambulance, amid the flurry of paramedics, running back and forth between their vehicle to what was left of the pickup, it was impossible to tell one man's sobs from the other.

It had been hours since a nurse or doctor had come out to update them on Julie's condition, and the waiting was taking its toll.

Lamont and Adam took turns pacing in the tiny, dark-carpeted space, stopping now and then outside the double doors leading to the surgical suite, while Nadine cuddled her sleeping granddaughter.

The elevator doors hissed open, and a tall, thin man stepped into the hall, balancing a drink holder on a big box of doughnuts. "Thought y'all might need somethin' to eat and drink," he said, depositing his gift on the round table in the center of the room.

Amy sat up and, stretching and yawning, climbed from Nadine's lap. "Hi, Mr. Jim!" she said, hugging his knees. "I haven't seen you in for*ever!*"

After saluting a silent hello to Adam and Lamont, he bent to make himself child-sized. "Been in Lubbock," he explained, "visiting my pa. Now, tell me, how's that purty mama of yours?"

She heaved a sad sigh. "The doctors are op'rating on her."

"Well, don't you worry none, li'l sweetie," he said, sitting beside Nadine, "she's gonna be fine, just fine." And after opening the doughnut box, he added, "Got two here just for you, chocolate with rainbow sprinkles."

Grinning, Amy looked at Nadine. "Can I have one, Grandmom?"

About an hour ago, she'd noticed that the sun, peeking through the slats of the miniblinds, had painted bright yellow stripes on the floor, announcing breakfast time for her early-rising grandchild. An egg bagel would have been a healthier, heartier breakfast, but Nadine didn't want to leave long enough to get one from the cafeteria. "Sure," she said with a wink.

She watched as Amy spread a paper napkin on the table, then sat on her knees, Japanese-style. "Mommy taught me this," she said with a nod, "to keep germs off my food." She looked at Jim. "Do you think I look like my mommy?"

"Yes, yes, I do."

She took a gigantic bite out of her doughnut, tilting her head and squinting one eye as she chewed. "Do you look like your mommy, too?"

Jim chuckled quietly. "Some people think so."

"You mean, your mother is *bald?*"

That drew a laugh from Nadine—from Lamont and Adam, too.

"Oh, no," Jim said, "my mama had a lot of hair. All the way down to her toes. Like a mermaid."

Amy's shoulders lifted in a dainty shrug. "Do you have a picture?"

"'Fraid not, li'l sweetie. At least, not here with me."

She put down her doughnut and slid a piece of white paper from her backpack. "Then I'll draw her for you," she said matter-of-factly. "Where does she live?"

"With the angels."

"You mean, you mean she's *dead?*"

"Yeah, but she was very, very old. It was time for her to be with Jesus."

Lamont and Adam had stopped pacing, Nadine noticed, to watch and listen to the interaction between Amy and the gentle giant. If she read their expressions correctly, they'd both changed their opinions of Jim. Or at the very least, reconsidered them. *Will wonders never cease?* she thought.

She stood to give Lamont and Adam a cup of the coffee Jim had brought, then put the juice box he'd bought Amy beside her drawing. She'd barely returned to her chair when the OR doors whooshed open and a bespectacled doctor burst into the waiting room, still wearing his surgical scrubs.

"Mr. Greene?" he asked, looking from face to anxious face.

"That's me," Adam said, extending a hand. "How's Julie?"

He took one look at Amy's haggard, wide-eyed face and said, "Is Julie your mommy?"

Both blond pigtails bobbed as she nodded.

"Well, you'll be happy to know that she's doing just fine. She's fast asleep right now, but you'll be able to see her in a day or two, okay?"

She looked up at Lamont. "Like when Obnoxious got poisoned?"

The doctor's brow furrowed.

"Sort of like that," Lamont said to Amy.

The surgeon signaled for Adam to follow him down the hall, and with a bob of his head, Adam signaled Nadine to come along.

"Your wife did very well," he said in hushed tones. He ran down the list of what procedures he and his team had performed—from relieving pressure on Julie's brain to draining blood that had collected in her chest cavity. "We had to put her on a ventilator, to help her breathe. In a few hours, we'll start weaning her off it, and if she does all right, we'll be able to move her to the ICU."

"When can I see her?"

"Right now, if you like. But I'll warn you, she's heavily sedated and attached to a lot of equipment. She won't even know you're there."

"I don't care," Adam said. "I just want to be with her." Then, "I, uh, you should probably know that she was diagnosed as a paranoid schizophrenic. Soon as she's able, I'll need to talk to someone about having her transferred to a facility that can get her on the right meds, make sure they're regulated. If I'd done that years ago, none of this would have happened."

"Mr. Greene—"

"Adam."

"Adam, it's been my experience that things like this happen, no matter how hard you work to prevent them. You won't do her or you or your little girl any good if you let yourself get all bogged down, trying to take the blame for something over which you had no control."

Nadine stepped closer and gave her boy a sideways hug, and he nodded.

"Well, I'll be checking in on her every few hours, so if you have any questions, don't hesitate to ask." He stretched. "I'll take you back to see her, and then I'm headed for the showers and a nice long nap in the doctors' lounge."

Adam faced Nadine. "I think I'm going to stay a while. No sense in all of you hanging around. Besides, Amy looks a little rough around the edges. Would you mind taking her home?"

She hugged him. "Don't you worry about a thing, sweetie. We'll be praying like crazy."

"I know." He sent her a thin smile. "Thanks, Mom."

And with that, he left Nadine alone to explain to Amy why she had to go home without her father… and without seeing her mother. *Lord,* she prayed, *be with me now…*

As the weeks passed, Nadine was forced to put her house on hold in order to help Adam and Amy, and hold up her end of the bargain with Lamont. And bless his big Texan heart, he never once made her feel rushed or put-upon. In fact, he'd taken to doing most of the shopping and cooking to help lighten her load.

Daily visits to the hospital were time-consuming and tiring, but she made a point of spending time with Julie, first thing in the morning or last thing at night. And, every day, Nadine saw small improvements that gave her hope that her daughter-in-law could soon be released to a psychiatric facility, where extensive testing and careful monitoring of medications would determine the best way to control her disorder. After that? Well, after that, God would guide them.

Shortly before her release from the hospital, the neurologist who'd treated her head injury asked permission to include Julie in a study he and his colleagues were conducting, to determine if massive head injury reduced or exacerbated the problems of schizophrenics. He ordered MRIs to study the different lobes of Julie's brain. His conclusions amazed everyone, including the renowned specialist himself.

"You see," Dr. Yadeen said, using his pen to point at the MRI results, "we most commonly find enlarged lateral ventricles, these fluid-filled sacs, here, around the brain." Blood flow, he explained, was usually lower in afflicted people, "and the temporal lobe tends to be smaller as well. This is important, since it is involved with sound, emotion and speech." He showed them past scans of Julie's brain, where vast differences were visible when comparing her brain scans to those of non-afflicted patients.

Next he showed them the most recent scans.

"As you can see, her prefrontal cortex—which is directly associated with memory—was severely impacted in the accident. I'm assuming she seemed somewhat scatterbrained beforehand?"

Adam nodded, and Nadine agreed.

"In the case of schizophrenics, dopamine receptors are—"

Adam stepped up to the viewing screen. "Whoa, Doc. Are you telling us that the accident might have *cured* her?"

The doctor shrugged. "This would appear to be the case, though it is entirely too early to tell for certain. With a brain injury of her severity, it's quite possible that things—if you'll pardon my American slang—were mashed and rearranged to the point that what *wasn't* transmitting before, *is* transmitting now, and the parts of her brain that once didn't send the proper signals, *are*."

"Like...like a miracle."

Another doctorly shrug. "I am a scientist and, as such, I do not believe in such things, Mr. Greene, but if that is an explanation you can live peacefully with, I'll not contradict it."

"Does that mean Julie won't need to be institutionalized?"

"For now, I'm quite comfortable in saying that you can take her home as soon as the rest of her doctors release her."

Adam slapped a palm to the back of his neck—exactly as Lamont did when he was confused or flustered. "It's all good news to me," he said, shaking the neurologist's hand.

"You're more than welcome to stay here in my office and study the films if you choose," the doctor said. "I'm afraid I have to go make my hospital rounds."

He left them sitting in stupefied silence, blinking and grinning and shaking their heads.

After several minutes, Adam got to his feet. "If you need me," he said, "I'll be with Julie, trying to figure out how to earn her forgiveness."

"There's nothing to forgive, son. How could you help her when you didn't know that anything was wrong?"

"Well, I guess it's a good thing for me that marriage is for a lifetime, then, isn't it?"

Nadine frowned. "I hate to be thickheaded, but I don't get it."

"I'll have years and years to make up for lost time." He gave her a big hug, then said, "You should go home, give Lamont a break, maybe take a nap with Amy."

Laughing, Nadine agreed. "Yeah, he's been on 'Amy Duty' a lot these days, hasn't he?"

She pictured the way he looked, sitting on the

floor as Amy clipped tiny pink barrettes in his dark hair. And as sat on a tiny chair, knees nearly touching his earlobes as he pretended to sip tea from a lavender cup that, in his big hands, looked like a thimble.

He'd hung coloring book pages on his fridge and displayed bunnies made from modeling clay on the corner of his mahogany desk. Her heart throbbed with love for the man who'd taught a frightened little girl how to make a fried bologna sandwich, and taught a lonely big girl the truth about the adage that "His bark is worse than his bite."

She walked with Adam to Julie's room, and after a short visit with them, headed for the hospital chapel. Like Adam, she felt an enormous desire to make things right between herself and Lamont. Hopefully, she prayed, she hadn't waited too long to ask for his forgiveness.

Nadine waited until the house was quiet, then tapped on Lamont's partially closed office door. How awful that because of her, he'd taken to holing up in here most evenings after supper.

"Yeah?"

Hopefully, what she'd come here to say would change all that. "It's just me," she said, shoving the door open just enough to slip into the room. "I thought you might like a cup of tea."

Lamont muted the tiny TV beside his desk. "Thanks." He put Julie's cat onto the floor, and as Peeper stalked off, singed tail flicking, Lamont cleared a space for the mug. "Funny, but I was just sitting here, thinking that it I wasn't such a lazy oaf, I'd get up and fix myself a cup." Grinning slightly, he added, "Because of you, my day just doesn't feel properly ended without one."

She grabbed a coaster and placed the mug in its center. "Am I interrupting anything important?"

"Nah." He turned off the television. "Unless you call listening to a couple of newsmen bicker something important. Where's your tea?"

"In the kitchen." She sat on the edge of one of the wingback chairs facing his desk. "I know it's late, but…" Nadine sure would love a sip of that tea right about now, not only to wet her parched throat, but as a stall tactic while she summoned her courage. "I was hoping that…" Eyes closed, she prayed for the Almighty's assistance.

He'd been leaning back in his big leather chair, ankles crossed and boot heels propped on the corner of his desk. One foot hit the floor, then the other, as he swiveled to face her.

Oh, what she'd give to erase the worried frown on his handsome brow, especially considering she'd painted it there. "I have something to tell you," she began, "and something to ask you. And neither will be easy for me, so I hope you'll let me get it all out before you say anything."

"Uh-oh," he ground out, "I don't like the way this is starting out…"

Nadine took a deep breath, then reached for his mug. "Sorry," she said, taking a sip, "but I'm more parched than the prairie."

He shrugged. "I meant it when I said what's mine is yours." One corner of his mouth lifted in a slight smile. "Right down to that."

His big gray eyes glittered with the truth of his words. Every moment spent in prayer these past weeks served to make her more and more certain that this was the man God had chosen for her. And if her unreasonable fears—carried to shield herself from possible heartache—hadn't messed things up beyond repair, she'd spend the rest of her days making it up to him. She cleared her throat. "I won't repeat my 'I'm so grateful I could pop' speech, because I know it upsets you. Instead, I'll start by saying I'm sorry…"

Nadine knew even as he opened his mouth that he aimed to tell her she had nothing to be sorry *for,* so she held up a hand to silence him. "I apologize for behaving like a childish little 'fraidy cat. I should have trusted you more. Trusted you sooner." Nadine took another sip of Lamont's tea. "Anyway," she continued, "you have my word, I'm one hundred percent finished with that nonsense. Permanently."

She almost wished she hadn't told him not to interrupt her. Almost. Because his cooperative silence only underscored how humbling it was, looking into eyes so filled with love, despite all she'd put him through.

Lamont wiggled his fingertips, then pointed at the tea. "Mind if I have a sip?"

"Oh." A nervous giggle popped from her lips. "Sorry." As she returned it to the coaster, her fingers grazed his. "It's probably not even hot anymore." Rising, she made a move to take it back. "Let me warm it up for you, and—"

"Let me hear your question instead, since it appears you've finished what you were going to tell me."

Lord, don't fail me now, she prayed, walking around the desk. Nadine knelt beside his chair and, fingers linked on his knee, looked up into his face. "I love you, Lamont, more than I've ever loved a man."

"I know."

Tears misted in her eyes. "You do?"

Nodding, he pulled her into his lap and kissed

the tip of her nose. "Please tell me that isn't your question."

She'd given this moment a lot of thought, a lot of planning, and a whole lot of prayer. Fingers trembling, Nadine slid a dented and tarnished ring from her shirt pocket.

"What. Is. *That?*" he asked, laughing softly.

"It's Amy's. She saved it from Lily's wedding reception. It was wrapped around the little parchment announcement beside each guest's plate, remember?"

He nodded. "Yes."

"I was hoping you'd say that."

His gaze slid from the ring to Nadine's face. "Say what?"

"Yes."

Lamont chuckled. "*That's* your question?"

"No."

He slapped a hand over his eyes. "Lord, shower me with patience." When he came out from hiding, he said, "Okay. I give up. What in the world are you talking about, pretty lady?"

"Remember that night in the kitchen, when you showed me that beautiful ring? The one your grandfather gave to your grandfather?"

"Yeah…"

"Well, I was insane to turn down your proposal."

She held up the tin band. "I'm hoping you won't be as crazy."

"Are you asking me to—"

"I thought at the time that saying no was in your best interest, because why would a handsome, successful rancher like you want to be saddled with a doddering old widow with more bills than brain cells, who was under suspicion of burning down her house, whose son and—"

"Nadine, neither of us is getting any younger."

"Y'know, when you're right, you're right." She dropped the cheap metal band into the palm of his left hand. "No way it'll fit on your big work-hardened ring finger, but remember, it's the thought that counts." Closing his fingers around it, Nadine whispered, "If you'll still have me, I'd love nothing more than to become your wife and spend the rest of my life with you."

For the next few seconds, the only sound in the room was the tick of a tiny pendulum, swinging to and fro inside the clock on his desk. Lamont's gaze flickered from her eyes to her lips and back again. "That was *not* a question."

"You're not going to make this easy on me, are you?"

Grinning mischievously, he shook his head. "Isn't every day an old cowpoke gets proposed to by a beautiful woman."

"Lamont London, will you marry me?"

"Darlin'," he said, holding her tight, "I thought you'd never ask."

Epilogue

Five years later

Lamont leaned back, one hand resting on the back of the porch swing, the other jingling ice cubes in a tall tumbler of lemonade.

Beyond the circular drive, a split-rail fence held a herd of fat, healthy heifers, the product of Nadine's massive Brahman bull. She'd given it to him the day after Julie had been released from the hospital, when he'd turned his living room into a hospital room, right down to the Y-bar attached to the beamed ceiling. "You can't expect me to just stand around with my hand out, 24/7," she'd said, "taking, taking, taking and never giving anything back!"

Little did she realize that, just by being part of his life, she'd given him more than he ever thought any man could hope for. Especially at his age!

And in the yard, Lily and Max with their four-year-old twins, Steven and Samantha, and Nate—who'd grown nearly as tall as his dad, playing horseshoes with Big Jim, almost as much a part of the family as the rest of them. Rosie—the little con artist—had talked the twins into playing a lopsided game of London Bridge. His own twins, Vi and Ivy, had flown in from Baltimore, each hoping time in their childhood home would help them heal from their respective heartbreaks. In the pool, Cammi and Reid played Marco Polo, rousing giggles from their baby boy, who bobbed beside them in a floating chair.

Sand buckets and soccer balls and badminton rackets littered the grass, while Obnoxious snored on a beach towel. Peeper snoozed on his lap, and beside him, looking more beautiful than she had on their wedding day, sat his wife.

"What are you grinning about, cowboy?"

"Just counting my blessings."

"I love having all the kids here, too. And with the family growing like it is, we have plenty of excuses to have them over to celebrate birthdays and anniversaries."

Today, it was Amy's turn to blow out the candles on a fanciful, thick-frostinged cake. "Hard to believe she's ten already," Lamont said. "Seems like only yesterday she was no bigger than a minute."

Nadine rested her head on his shoulder. "I know. Time sure flies when you're having fun."

He wondered how many clichés she'd quoted over the years. Thousands? Hundreds of thousands? Chuckling, he kissed her temple. "Happy?"

"Very."

"Even though we canceled our trip to the islands?"

She looked into his face. "To tell you the truth, Caribbean cruises are great, but…" She waved at Rosie, who now had her twin cousins rolling down the slope that led to the gazebo. "I'd much rather celebrate our fifth anniversary—*all* our anniversaries—right here on River Valley soil. Besides, you couldn't *drag* me that far from home with another grandbaby on the way."

"I feel the same way."

She cuddled closer and kissed his cheek. "Y'big softie…"

Odd, how things turned out, he thought, nodding to himself. About the time everything that was upside down turned right-side up, the insurance check arrived, and Nadine used it to build a two-story cottage on the foundation of her old house. As the contractor was nailing the final shingles to the roof, she'd asked Lamont what he'd say if she decided to rent the place.

"I'd say you're nuts," he'd said. "Do you really

want to be a landlady, getting calls in the middle of the night because the toilet's stopped up or the furnace isn't working?"

That's when she'd showed him the gigantic greeting card she and Amy had made to welcome Adam and Julie home from their second honeymoon, in which she'd tucked the deed to the cottage.

It was a great idea, he'd said. His girls were settled in homes of their own, and he and Nadine were happy here at River Valley. Julie's recovery had been nothing short of miraculous, and it would be good having the kids close, so they could help Adam make sure she stayed that way.

"Gra-a-n-da-a-ad," Amy sing-songed, "you pro-o-mi-i-issed…"

Nadine laughed. "Better grab your towel, mister, 'cause I don't think you're gonna wriggle out of doing the belly flop this time."

"I suppose you're right," he said. "But if I'm not back in fifteen minutes, send in the SWAT team."

"How 'bout if I just call you all in for dinner, instead?" She wrinkled her nose. "That'd be a lot less fuss and bother, don't you think?"

Laughing, Lamont said, "Yeah, I guess we've had more than our share of visits from the Amarillo emergency crews."

Standing, he leaned forward to leave the swing, and she grabbed his hand. "What about you, Lamont? Are you happy?"

"Happier than I've ever been." And to prove it, he punctuated the statement with a long, loving kiss.

"I have something for you," she said softly, "an anniversary present. But you can't open it until later, after all the kids have gone home."

"I don't need a gift," he said, kissing her again. "Everything I need is right here."

"But Lamont, I—"

He gestured toward the yard, where their kids and grandkids frolicked. "You gave me *that*." Then he gently chucked her chin. "And you gave me *this*. I doubt I could handle any more joy."

Bracketing his face with both hands, she touched the tip of her nose to his. "I suppose you're right. We did sort of—"

"Oh, Granddad," Amy called again. She stood on the diving board, wagging her forefinger. "It isn't nice to break promises to birthday girls…"

"All right," he said, putting Peeper on the ground. "But stand back, because you're about to see the biggest belly flop in the history of the River Valley swimming pool."

The feline aimed a flat-eyed glare at him, then walked away, tail flicking.

"It appears that she resents having her cozy lap taken away so abruptly," Julie said, picking up the cat. "And don't pay a bit of attention to that silly daughter of mine." She patted her round belly. "It's high time she got used to sharing her grandfather—and everything else."

Lamont winked. "She's gonna be an A-1 big sister. Just you wait and see."

Laughing, his daughter-in-law put the cat inside, and slid the screen door closed behind her. "You'd think after all these years, I wouldn't still be miffed at you for stealing my little Peeper."

"Hey, I tried to give her back. Couple hundred times."

She kissed the top of his head. "Well, you have no one but yourself to blame."

"Hey, wait just a cotton pickin' minute, here..." Lamont said.

"That's what having a heart as big as Texas will get you."

"What?"

"You saved my life. Twice, by my count."

"Jules," he began, "you're—"

"I don't think I need to remind you what you said that night, when I was so willing to let go. If you hadn't stood there, nagging and hammering at me."

Lamont looked at Nadine. "You think she knows how good she is at deflating a bloated ego?"

The threesome laughed. Then Julie pointed into the yard, where bright helium-filled balloons and colorful streamers danced on a sultry Texas breeze, and a spritely tune thumped from a boom box.

"What you get when your heart is as big as Texas is grandkids and daughters-in-law who think you hung the moon, and pets that adopt *you*..." Julie said, as Peeper meowed on cue.

"...and you wind up the head of a big, happy, accidental family."

Nadine smiled. "...and you end up as the head of a big, happy, accidental family."

* * * * *

Dear Reader,

Genesis is chock-full of "family stories," including the legendary account of Cain and Abel. No doubt Adam and Eve were heartbroken by the tragic rift between their boys. But can you imagine how much more horrible they would have felt if siblings and in-laws gathered 'round to share "I told you so's"!

Families give us much to celebrate—births and birthdays, weddings and anniversaries, graduations, job promotions and retirement. And they give us cause to mourn, too, when a loved one is diagnosed with cancer, a marriage dies, or a child bends to the temptation of drugs. Grandkids break bones. Husbands have heart attacks. Parents slip into the fog of Alzheimer's.

We can count on our families for little joys, such as the greeting cards that arrive like clockwork from a sister who lives in distant state, or the brief "I was thinking about you!" email from the brother who hates gabbing on the phone. And for balance, there's the brother-in-law who routinely arrives late for Thanksgiving dinner, and the nephew who delights in making the toilet overflow every single time he visits!

For people like Nadine Greene and Lamont

London—each with their own up-down, happy-sad, good-bad "relative moments"—blending *two* families is a challenge, to say the least. But to find their second chance at love amid all the chaos? Good thing they had the promise of their Heavenly Father to see them through to their happy ending, wasn't it!

I pray that in your own family, joy will far outweigh heartache, and that when hard times befall you or your loved ones, you'll always find comfort in the promise of the Father: "…and then I will welcome you, and I will be a father to you, and you will be my sons and daughters, says the Lord Almighty." (2 Corinthians 6:18)

Now that you've finished reading *An Accidental Family,* I hope you'll tell me all about your favorite part of the story. You can write me at loree@loreelough.com or c/o Love Inspired Books, 233 Broadway, New York, NY 10279. (I love hearing from readers, and try to answer every letter, personally!)

Blessings to you and yours,

Loree Lough

QUESTIONS FOR DISCUSSION

1. What expectations did you have for Lamont and Nadine's relationship when they first met?

2. List three of Nadine's "issues" with Lamont.

3. And what are his "issues" with her?

4. What were Lamont's most admirable character strengths?

5. His weaknesses?

6. What did you like best about Nadine?

7. What do you consider her major flaw?

8. Why did Nadine have such a hard time admitting her "relationship fears"?

9. Do you feel that Lamont behaved appropriately toward Julie and Adam?

10. Which of the two main characters did *you* most closely identify with? Why?

11. Who's your favorite secondary character? Why?

12. If you had to select one "faith theme" from this novel, what would it be?

LARGER-PRINT BOOKS!

**GET 2 FREE
LARGER-PRINT NOVELS
PLUS 2 FREE
MYSTERY GIFTS**

Love Inspired®

Larger-print novels are now available...

Love Inspired®
SUSPENSE
RIVETING INSPIRATIONAL ROMANCE

Watch for our series of edge-
of-your-seat suspense novels.
These contemporary tales
of intrigue and romance
feature Christian characters
facing challenges to their faith...
and their lives!

**AVAILABLE IN REGULAR
& LARGER-PRINT FORMATS**

For exciting stories that reflect traditional values,
visit:
www.ReaderService.com